HOUSE OF SHADOWS

Borgo Press Books by EVELYN BOND

House of Shadows: A Gothic Novel of Terror

HOUSE OF SHADOWS

A GOTHIC NOVEL OF TERROR

EVELYN BOND

Edited by Mary Wickizer Burgess

THE BORGO PRESS

MMXII

HOUSE OF SHADOWS

FIRST BORGO PRESS EDITION

Published by Wildside Press LLC

www.wildsidebooks.com

HOUSE OF SHADOWS

CONTENTS

PART ONE 9

CHAPTER ONE 10

CHAPTER TWO 20

CHAPTER THREE 23

CHAPTER FOUR 37

CHAPTER FIVE 49

CHAPTER SIX .67

PART TWO 77

CHAPTER SEVEN 78

CHAPTER EIGHT 88

CHAPTER NINE 99

CHAPTER TEN 109

CHAPTER ELEVEN 125

CHAPTER TWELVE 131

PART THREE 141

CHAPTER THIRTEEN 142

CHAPTER FOURTEEN 147

CHAPTER FIFTEEN 154

CHAPTER SIXTEEN 175

CHAPTER SEVENTEEN 184

ABOUT THE AUTHOR 192

PART ONE

CHAPTER ONE

Much later, she recalled that night in perfect detail with intense longing, wanting to turn back the clock to a more carefree existence. Amidst the difficult months that followed, during the heart of the accusations and turmoil and violent death that never seemed to end, during the worst of the terror that would fill so many of her future nights, Laura was still able to recall that one perfect evening—and to smile as she did so. She did wonder, at times, if she should have realized back then just how uncertain her future really was. She'd been naive, she now knew, and terribly, terribly foolish in so many ways. And yet, at the start of the particular night in question, she'd been so cheerful, so happy, so pleasantly excited at the possibilities. It all happened, she thought, such a *very* long time ago....

* * * * * * *

Laura Foster stood in her tiny apartment kitchen and gazed down at the ingredients laid out before her. A lock of otherwise well-trained bright blonde hair swooped down in front of one blue eye, but the pretty young girl was too deeply absorbed to push it back.

"No peppercorns," she said at last, glancing in exasperation at a slightly older brunette also contemplating the defrosted duckling waiting to be braised in the next hour or so. "You forgot to bring the peppercorns."

Rochelle Stoddard sighed. "I should hope your boyfriend's

palate can get along without peppercorns."

"He's not just a boyfriend!" The trace of a smile stretched Laura's full, warm lips. "You know what I'm expecting from him tonight!"

"Well, I certainly hope he does propose," Rochelle said, looking quizzically at her friend. "I haven't even met him yet, whoever he is."

"His name is Felix Page, as you well know, and he's a brilliant architect—and I hope he's going to be my—my—"

Laura couldn't make herself say the magic word, but it trembled between the two young friends in the evening air of the overheated kitchen. She turned away and took off the flowered apron she'd been wearing, tossing it across a nearby chair.

Rochelle gave a puzzled frown. "What are you doing, honey? You haven't even started to cook this darned bird."

"I've got to go out and get the peppercorns, thanks to you."

"Are you kidding? I heard a rumor that we're living in the enlightened era now. Nobody in her right mind should go out of her way just to show off for some man."

"I'm *not* showing off," Laura said, leaving the kitchen on her way to the hall closet. "But I want Felix to know that I'm a really good cook."

"It's not a point you're ever going to have to prove, in my opinion. If this fellow's got as much dough as you say he does, you'll be on easy street, with a cook and servants of your own." Rochelle followed her into the entryway.

"But don't you see?" Laura said earnestly. "It's important that he knows I understand the finer points of good cuisine. After all, even if we have a cook, I'll need to know if she's doing a good job, won't I?"

"Whatever.... Come to think of it, you haven't mentioned anything else all week at rehearsals except for 'Felix this' and 'Felix that.' I know I'm just panting to get a chance to meet such a 'boy wonder'—this Felix whatever-his-name is—"

"Felix *Page*, Ro. His name is Felix Page—and of course you'll meet him—eventually."

"As a matter of fact, one reason I volunteered to help with this culinary orgy of yours tonight is just so I could finally get a peek at him."

Laura stopped in the midst of pulling on her winter coat to check the contents of her wallet. "The problem is that Felix is—well, I suppose you could call him shy. Nobody would expect that from a man of the world who has to deal with other people all the time, both in society and in his business. But he truly is. And he's very—well, you'll see for yourself, sooner or later, Ro. Now I'm just going to run downstairs to the market. I'll be back in a few minutes and we can get started on the duck."

She had cut short of saying that Felix Page could be quick-tempered. It was true, but she didn't want anybody, especially Rochelle, to think she might be criticizing her dream man. And yet it was impossible to be with Felix for any length of time and not get the impression that he was struggling to control a disposition toward fierce and implacable anger.

Just recently, in fact, his temper had erupted during a disagreeable incident in a night club. They were dancing, when she suddenly felt the muscles of his left arm tighten.

"Is something wrong?" she asked.

"Our waiter has been so rude and inattentive that I'd like to punch him until he can't see straight."

"Well, the place is very busy tonight, and you can't know what kind of strain he's been under."

"I'm under a worse strain because of him."

"Well, if that's how you feel, you should go ahead and punch him and work the inhibitions out of yourself," she said lightly, attempting to make a joke of the situation.

Felix had thrown back his head and laughed. "Is that what you learned in drama school, Laura? To forget all your inhibitions and do exactly what you want?"

Laura said quietly, "I was thinking about what *you* want."

Felix looked at her then, as if for the first time. He smiled, and she could feel the tension melting from his arm muscles.

Felix Page *was* quick-tempered, as she'd nearly told her friend

Rochelle just now; but, she added to herself silently, he could be soothed and calmed down by the right woman. And Laura knew that she was the right woman for Felix Page. She knew it with a compelling intensity that would not be denied.

She left the apartment at twenty minutes to seven, and promptly discovered that the West Seventies area of Manhattan, on a windy January night in 1965, wasn't the easiest place in the world in which to buy peppercorns. The first store reluctantly sent her to a competitor across the street which, it turned out, did not have them either. She finally took a taxi to a specialty store on Broadway, wishing all the while she had done just that when she had started out on her travels.

There she realized that, by the time she paid for the cab, she hadn't brought quite enough money with her. The manager, eager to close, took pity on the pretty blonde's distress and gave her the peppercorns anyway, nodding cheerfully at Laura's promise to pay it back the next day—and to become a steady customer for as long as she'd be keeping an apartment in the general neighborhood. Unlike many young actresses, Laura intended to keep her promise.

As she unlocked her apartment door again at seven-fifteen, she heard Rochelle's distinctive voice, ringing out clearly in what she sometimes called her "stage manner." When Rochelle stopped speaking she was answered briefly by a man.

With the container of peppercorns in one hand, Laura rushed into the living room.

"You're early!" she said.

Felix Page stood to greet her. Light from the single lamp in the small, neat room reflected the sheen of his dark hair and the tan of his chiseled face. Bright blue eyes darted from her to Rochelle—and back to Laura again, in obvious relief.

"You're an hour too soon!" Laura said accusingly. "I've hardly begun the cooking. What made you decide to come so early, Felix?"

"I didn't have anything better to do," he said with a smile.

Rochelle made a move to get up. "Well, now that you're back,

Laura, I *suppose* I ought to leave."

She had been sitting turned away from the door, and she did not look up when Laura entered. She seemed fascinated by Felix, who, in his turn, was looking away from her, in Laura's direction, so that Rochelle was unable to see his face clearly in the shadows.

"I can take a little walk and come back later," he offered.

"Whatever you like, Felix," Laura said. "But don't let either of us chase you out of here."

"Do you know something, honey?" Rochelle suddenly turned toward Laura. "I think I've seen Felix before somewhere, but I can't quite remember the time or place."

"You probably saw me at some party or other," Felix said brusquely. "I was in New York a few years ago and met quite a few people then."

His voice wasn't exactly out of control, but he appeared to be fighting off an outburst of temper, and the effort showed plainly in the clenched, white-knuckled fists he held stiffly at his sides.

"No. I think it was more recent than that. I'll probably think of it when I'm on stage tomorrow," Rochelle said. "Maybe you were my fourth husband or something!"

Rochelle had never been married, Laura knew, and she had no idea what would cause her to make such a stupid remark about the brief duration of some marriages. Her "friend" was probably amusing herself at Laura's expense, she thought disgustedly.

"You should go see Rochelle on stage sometime, Felix," Laura said, attempting to change the subject. "She's quite good. Right now she's rehearsing the lead role in that murder-mystery, *The Trial of Mary Dugan*, and even though the play is a little dated, you'd never know it from Rochelle's take on it."

"You're such a dear for saying so, Laura," Rochelle murmured. Her voice gathered even more strength and vibrancy in response to the compliment. "But I'd still like to know where I've seen Felix before. There aren't that many dark, handsome men in New York that I'd forget even one of them."

Felix seemed very uncomfortable with Rochelle's continued

attention, but Laura didn't really want to send him out in the cold weather to take a walk. On the other hand, Rochelle, she could sense, was enjoying his discomfort, and probably would resist leaving the apartment by any method short of force.

"Why don't you turn on the TV while I'm cooking?" Laura grasped for a solution to her dilemma. "At least then I'll know that you two are enjoying yourselves—while I'm out here working my fingers to the bone."

"You sound like a sweet little house *frau* already," Rochelle said maliciously. "Trying to get in character?"

Felix, jaw set, turned abruptly away from the women and switched on the set, settling down in a deep chintz easy chair with his back toward Rochelle's probing eyes.

Laura returned to the kitchen and the duck-to-be-braised, hoping for no more trouble from what she had already begun to think of as the "living room crisis." There was nothing like an audience to bring out the viciousness in Rochelle. Even with her generosity of spirit, her friend could be quite mean-spirited, Laura knew, particularly when the subject under discussion was a rival for attention. A mutual friend of theirs, having heard Rochelle's snarky opinion of another actress, had labeled Rochelle a "perfumed and powdered viper."

Laura had finished cutting up the duck and was drying the pieces preparatory to popping them in a sizzling pan, when she realized that the television had been abruptly shut off. As she gingerly raised one of the spattering duck pieces with a spatula, she heard Felix's voice raised in anger.

She dropped the spatula, quickly turned down the fire, and wiped both hands on a towel. As she turned in apprehension to the kitchen door, it opened abruptly on Rochelle, who stepped inside, rigid with anger. She raised an imperious forefinger and pointed back at the door angrily.

"Don't you dare marry him," she growled. "Even if he gets down on his knees and begs you, don't. It'd be a lot smarter to kick him out right now—and throw that blasted duck, peppercorns and all, after him."

"If you don't like Felix," Laura said briskly, "then I'm afraid that's your problem."

"'Like'? All I did was ask the man where I had seen him before, and he keeps telling me not to bother him. Finally I told him I'd just look for his picture on the wall the next time I was in the post office. It was only a joke, but I swear he made a rush for me as if he was going to—"

Felix Page burst into the kitchen. His face was red and drawn under the glare of lights in the tiny over-heated room. He looked angry, whether he was or not. He continued pulling on his jacket, licked his lips carefully and then blurted out:

"I'm leaving now...."

"I don't want you to go," Laura said in a calmer tone than she felt. "I think that the both of you have been acting like a pair of spoiled brats; especially you, Rochelle."

"Yes, I was sure you'd think it was my fault." Rochelle had taken a couple of steps backward when Felix entered, and now she stood huddled next to Laura by the stove. She hadn't taken her eyes off him, and there was an uncharacteristic edge of fear in her eyes. For once, Laura thought, in the naïveté of her twenty-three years, Rochelle looks a lot older than I do.

"Look. No matter whose fault it is, let's just let it go and relax," Laura said. "I don't want the two of you at each other's throats. Rochelle, if you'd just change the subject, I'm sure that the two of you can get along well enough and let me finish the cooking."

"In other words, if I just play it like something out of Oscar Wilde." Rochelle forced herself to smile and altered her voice slightly: 'My, isn't this cold weather just *ruining* your Florida tan, Mr. Page?'"

Felix didn't respond. He stood silently, fists clenched; his breathing seemed ragged.

"No. I don't think there's a thing that will work with your friend—except for a pair of handcuffs," Rochelle said. "Honey, it'll be a whole lot easier for all of us right now if I just make my getaway—exit stage left."

Laura, who had been wishing Rochelle would leave on her own, hoped her relief wasn't too obvious. "Nobody's forcing you to go," she said pointedly.

"*That's* a matter of opinion," Rochelle said. "But when I leave, it'll only be good for your peace of mind tonight, not in the long run."

Laura could hardly keep from telling her irksome friend that she was going to be only too happy to find out what was going to happen to her peace of mind in the weeks and months and years that lay ahead.

"There's one other thing I want to tell you here and now—and in present company—especially in present company," Rochelle added quietly.

Laura felt a sudden tightening in her chest, as if she had put on a jacket that was several sizes too small. "We'll be seeing each other tomorrow, as usual," she said. "The two of us can talk about it then."

"No!" Rochelle paused, and then controlled her voice to sound unhurried and reflective. "No. I know people think I'm mean and sarcastic—and maybe I am. But I'm trying my best not to be either of those things right now. Do you understand me, honey?"

Laura nodded.

"Look, honey, you're just a kid. You're all of twenty-three years old. You have no parents and no relatives, so there isn't anybody you can go to who'll say what he or she really thinks about this boyfriend of yours. You want to become attached to somebody and you want to hold on to a man who'll be part of your life forever. I can understand that, and I sympathize. Believe me, Laura, I can see it from your angle."

Rochelle paused. Her eyes hadn't left Felix at any time, but now they grew steely.

"He's not the one for you. This fellow has got the most vicious temper I've ever seen in my life, and believe me I've been around a bit longer—and seen a bit more—than you have. When the two of you have any kind of argument (and you're bound to, heaven knows), this one here is mean enough to put his hands on your throat and squeeze the li—"

Laura could never be sure exactly how it happened. One moment Felix was glaring at Rochelle, hands taut and clenched at his sides. In the next moment he started to say something, couldn't bring out the words he wanted, and raised both hands. He had been leaning forward, but Laura never knew whether or not he took a step toward Rochelle.

Rochelle, though, moved as if her worst fears had come to life in front of her. She pulled back abruptly against the stove. The skillet shifted to one side. There was a sound of inhuman whistling, and then, with a metallic thump, the pan jumped off the stove, unceremoniously dumping darkened wedges of duck meat—and peppercorns—all over the floor.

"Oh Lord, honey, I'm so sorry," Rochelle said. She had recovered her poise when Felix stepped back in surprise at the harsh sounds from the stove. "All that work, and what you get for it is a lot of dirty linoleum."

Laura managed to say something innocuous as she walked her friend to the closet to retrieve her coat, and then to the door. Rochelle was quiet for once, probably trying to think of a good exit line. Laura's suspicion of this was confirmed at the door. There, Rochelle glanced back at Laura, and, apparently referring to the play about a murder trial which they were currently rehearsing, said lightly:

"So long, honey, and *I'll see you in court.*"

When Laura returned to the kitchen she saw that Felix was gravely at work, picking up the duck pieces and carefully laying them on a paper towel across the dinette table.

"I think you can save it," he said, avoiding her eyes. "Or maybe someone you know has a dog and can use the meat...."

"You're probably right," Laura said. The destruction of her evening's hopes was weighing on her, now that the shock was over; but she didn't want to make Felix even more uncomfortable by continuing to talk about it. "I guess I could open some cans for tonight; that's what I usually do."

"No. Let's have dinner out," Felix suggested. "What happened here was my fault, so the least I can do is make it up to you a little bit."

Laura now was convinced, with a sinking heart, that there would be no marriage proposal from Felix Page tonight. Under the circumstances, though, there was nothing for her to do except give in to his wishes gracefully.

"All right. I guess that would be best."

"Good. I'll call and see if it's not too late to reserve a table at the Miami Restaurant. I've been meaning to try it. At least the name has an association with my home state! And I think I'd appreciate that, tonight. This may be a special occasion after all."

Laura tried to tell herself that he still meant to propose marriage tonight, even though he continued to stand and look at her awkwardly, as if he were embarrassed by something.

"May I use your phone?"

"Yes, of course."

After he had left the kitchen, she suddenly realized that he had been hesitating to ask to use her phone because it was located in her bedroom! He was shyness incarnate, she guessed, even though he had made at least two furious rushes at Rochelle Stoddard tonight. Laura began to believe that no matter how long she might live, she would never be able to understand what made this man tick.

CHAPTER TWO

The Miami Restaurant was crowded in spite of the late hour, as Felix had anticipated it would be. He and Laura finally were led to a table behind a potted plant near the kitchen—and they took it because there was no better choice. Felix was muttering under his breath as he sat down, but then shrugged it off and asked Laura to tell him a little more about herself, adding that he didn't know as much about Laura's background as he'd like.

So Laura told him what it had been like to be raised in a succession of foster homes after her parents' untimely deaths, and of how she was drawn to a stage career as a way, she supposed, of attracting some attention to herself, a way of proving her worth to all those foster parents.

"And is this the kind of work you expect to keep on doing indefinitely?" Felix asked.

"I doubt if acting is an older woman's profession, unless you become extremely famous. It's the sort of career a young girl goes into on the assumption that she won't have to worry for too long about working," she laughed. "Hopefully, some man will marry her and take that particular problem off her shoulders!"

Felix was about to reply to that when the waiter came to serve the soup. He began instead to talk casually about the design of the restaurant, and it led him into a more general discussion of his favorite topic, architecture. Over the past few months, since they met, he had been teaching Laura the joy of looking at a building for its own sake, and both his diffidence and his anger seemed to vanish as he enlarged on the subject closest to his heart.

He had begun telling her how he would have recast the cavernous restaurant if he were designing it, when he glanced toward the kitchen and suddenly growled:

"I hope the main dish will be a hell of a lot better than this soup."

"I expect it will," Laura said soothingly.

The waiter returned with a cheerful apology for having taken such a long time about the service. He was an older man, and his uniform was immaculate.

Felix took a bite of the meat and promptly spat it out. The waiter looked patiently at Felix, who tapped the cloth-covered tabletop.

"This is overdone," he said finally. "I ordered it rare."

"Would you like me to take it back, sir?"

"Of course. I'm not going to—never mind. Take it back."

When the waiter was gone again, Felix said, "It's like eating in one of those motels that have sprung up in Florida like a plague. But I swear that not one of those cheap tinhorn nature-destroyers is going to be put up in El Norte. Not one."

"Have you lived in El Norte long?"

"It's my home—a pristine strip of Florida coastline and absolutely glorious," he said. "My mother, my half-brother, and I have been there for as long as I can remember, and I'm sure that as soon as you—"

The waiter now returned with the rare steak, and made a point of standing at the table until Felix had tasted it and admitted that it was now fit to eat.

He cleared his throat when the waiter had moved on, and said haltingly, "I was going to say that as soon as you—ah—can visit the place you'll see why I like it so much."

Laura knew perfectly well what he had actually wanted to say, if it had not been for the night's succession of unlucky accidents, but she hoped her disappointment didn't show.

Felix leaned forward earnestly. "Listen here, Laura. My job in New York is over, and the building will be ready for occupancy on Friday, so the two of us could fly down to El Norte. You could stay for the weekend, chaperoned by my mother, and you could return here on Sunday night. How's that? Will you be my guest?"

"I—why, yes, I'd be happy to spend a few days down there," she said.

"Good, Laura, I'm very glad." He swallowed part of his coffee and made a face. "Let me take you to a little espresso place I know where the coffee is good and the waiter brings what you ask for."

But she couldn't help but notice that, in spite of all his complaints, he left a generous tip. For the second time that evening, Laura wondered if she would ever understand this man.

The next morning she returned to the drafty rehearsal hall and asked to speak to the director. "I have to catch an early flight this afternoon, Bill. I can't stay for rehearsals. I'm sorry."

The director shrugged. "That's all right, kid, we can work around you. Good luck on your trip, by the way—and be sure to take care of yourself."

She glanced from the director to Rochelle, who had been standing quietly in the wings awaiting her cue. "Do you mean anything in particular by that?"

"Naw—I just don't want anything happening to you," Bill said. "I know the kind of trouble a kid like you can get into. You're the sort who adopts stray cats and lame dogs— ain'tcha'?—one of the innocent-bystander types who walks into a bad scene with eyes wide open, then can't figure out why she's the only one who got hurt. Like I said, Laura, *take care of your-self.*" His words echoed in her ears as she rushed to pick up her luggage and meet Felix at the airport.

It was odd, in retrospect, that at that moment she had no sense at all of the malevolent presence—calmly and inexorably, awaiting their arrival in El Norte.

CHAPTER THREE

Laura was uncomfortably warm in her heavy winter suit as soon as she stepped off the plane into the steamy Florida heat. Felix, darkly handsome in a more appropriate white linen suit, went off to flag down a cab and phone his mother that they had arrived safely and would be at the house shortly. She was watching all the people walking back and forth along the glazed floor in the terminal, when she suddenly realized something else was making her anxious: it was the knowledge that she and Felix had been unnecessarily rude to Rochelle. Here she was, relaxing in the warm sun during January, while her friends and colleagues were all trapped in the throes of a vicious New York winter. There was a certain indecency to it. And, she told herself ruefully, a short weekend in this climate might actually bring on a nasty cold when she went back to her wintry home.

Felix reappeared at the end of the long, brightly-lit corridor and gestured for her to follow him. She did, and soon found herself in the back seat of a wide, comfortable cab.

Felix gazed out the window for some five minutes after the cab was under way, as if he was reacquainting himself with his surroundings. Laura caught part of his fierce muttered comment:

"...every damn week."

"Excuse me?"

"I said that I think there must be more of *those* in the area every damn week."

Laura looked past his shaking finger. A huge, brightly-colored billboard was placed in the midst of a verdant parkway, lush with swaying palms, and a spread-out three-story motel and its parking lot, garish in pink stucco with a flamingo on its blinking sign, flashed past, blocking off the view of the shore and ocean beyond. One after another, a fast-food stand, a souvenir shop, a gas station, and a diner advertising "Florida-burgers," whatever they were, quickly followed suit.

"These developers seem determined to pollute God's perfection," Felix said. "Why on earth can't these places be contained in one separate enclave and the rest of the area be left alone?"

"I suppose because it isn't businesslike to do it any other way," she said thoughtfully.

"And damn few people care enough about it to fight." He struck his kneecaps with clenched fists. "Well, I care enough. My family has lived in El Norte for a hundred years, and I'm not going to see it befouled like so much of the rest of this country."

The driver, a thick-necked Cuban in a white cap, suddenly chuckled.

Felix, his eyes narrowing, glared at what was visible of the man's back. "Do you think I'm wrong, driver?"

"No, it isn't that." The driver spoke in a subdued voice that wasn't far from being a whisper. His tan hands rested lightly but firmly on the bone-white wheel. "I'm sure you'll do the best you can, *señor*, to keep the developers out of El Norte...."

"But you think I won't be able to prevent it, is that your point?"

"Well, *señor*, I see it like this: El Norte has got plenty of rich people living in it, or else it'd already have been sliced up like a melon. Just the same, it covers about a hundred and fifty miles of coastline. You don't suppose that the investors are gonna pass all that by, *señor*, now do you?"

"El Norte will fight the developers in every court there is, and start up some lynching parties afterwards if need be."

"I don't think you'll win that battle. The developers have got all the time in the world and you locals can't keep up the same pitch of anger or pride forever. Do you see what I mean?"

"No, I think you're wrong." There was a grayish-white line

forming around Felix's mouth; he was obviously frustrated at not being able to argue a point he felt so strongly about, particularly with a cab-driver.

"Well, it's probably been a while since you were here, hasn't it? A couple months, maybe, *señor*?"

Felix was now so tense that Laura put out a restraining hand to keep him from leaning any closer to the driver. Felix gave no indication that he noticed her or even felt her hand on his arm.

"What about it? Why are you asking how long I've been away?"

"Because in the last couple of months—oh, oh! We're coming into El Norte now and I'd better slow down a bit."

"What's happened in the last few months?" Felix insisted.

There was no response from the driver, who had turned his attention to a complex set of turns. Felix smacked his palm flush against the back of the front seat. The driver, startled, lost control for a moment, and the cab swayed briefly as it started up a rise along a ridge. Frustrated, Felix sat back in his seat, and the driver continued on up the road.

It was Laura's first sight of El Norte and, at last, she thought she understood how Felix felt about preserving it from development. She saw a swatch of clean blue sky providing a brilliant backdrop against a series of reddish earthen bluffs. Farther out towards the horizon, the mighty ocean pounded unrelentingly against the long sandy shore. Bright green palm trees and a long narrow swath of grass dotted with beds of tropical flowers bordered the drive on either side. Laura opened her window to let in the perfumed breeze and realized that she had never known a sensation quite like it. The balmy air smelled like some nectar of the gods.

"Felix," she said quietly, "this is—wonderful, just wonderful. I think I know now exactly what you meant."

He hadn't been listening. All his energies were centered on the driver's swarthy face reflected in the rearview mirror. He spoke clearly and carefully just before the cab reached a more level stretch of road:

"I want to know what you're hinting at about El Norte."

"Why, it's really a lot more simple than you'd think," the driver said after a pause. "There's a proposition up before the State Highway Commission to—here we are!"

Laura was concentrated entirely on Felix, who sat with an ear actually cupped to hear the words more clearly. His lips moved, but no words came out. Gradually her attention was drawn to their surroundings. A huge old house in Victorian style, its shingles and siding freshly painted a sparkling off-white, loomed over an ornate circular, brick-paved courtyard where their cab had drawn up and parked beneath a shady *porte-cochère*.

As they got out of the cab, a pair of tall wooden doors, brightly painted in turquoise, opened wide, and, as Laura watched in curiosity, a dark-featured man, a little older, and a little heavier, than Felix, stepped out of the shadowy interior. He waved both hands at the new arrivals and ran awkwardly toward them.

"What *about* the Highway Commission?" Felix was demanding insistently of the driver. "Do they want to put new roads through El Norte itself?"

"No new roads," the driver assured Felix as he swung open the trunk and began pulling out their luggage. "But it's near the same thing, if you ask me. They're planning to—"

He was interrupted by the newcomer who was jumping up and down and calling out gleefully: "Felix! Felix!" Laura was reminded suddenly of a small child greeting an adult in hopes that a toy has been brought as a gift.

Seen up close, the child-man, his eyes gleaming with warmth and friendliness, looked much older than Felix, and the chiseled features that had made the one face so compelling to Laura, seemed to have been blurred and softened in this other, similar, countenance. Surely he wasn't more than thirty-five years old, yet, in some ways, he seemed ancient. A crooked smile tugged at the corners of his fleshy lips, and a fleck of spittle marred an otherwise pristine appearance.

Felix held up one hand to prevent his half-brother from interrupting his train of thought.

"The Highway Commission is considering new plans," the driver said finally when he realized Felix was still waiting for a response to his question. "They want to build a new super highway right through this area, much wider than the existing route. That probably means they're expecting a lot more traffic and, it's just my opinion of course, but I think it's the beginning of the end for El Norte, as a quiet little burg, I mean."

Felix whirled on his half-brother who cringed and staggered back, as if he expected to be swatted. "Is anybody doing anything about this, Harvey?"

Harvey shrugged vaguely. "About what, Felix? I just came out to get your bags."

Felix, muttering to himself, nearly knocked Harvey down in his haste to get to the front door. Without bothering to apologize he jerked it open so violently that one of the large wooden hurricane shutters affixed to one side of the double doors drifted loose and swayed back and forth in a semicircle, like some ancient signaling device.

The house itself, now that Laura took a moment to look at it, was a huge multi-story affair with several wings and a wide balcony splayed across the second floor supported by the *porte-cochère* below. It looked as though it had been standing there, unchanged, for many years, and it wouldn't have surprised her to find no signs of modernization on the inside at all.

But she was wrong. Walking in ahead of the hard-breathing Harvey who was laboring from the weight of the luggage, which he had insisted on carrying alone, Laura found herself in a spacious, yet comfortably-furnished foyer. She was particularly attracted to a handsome pair of vintage portraits, obviously husband and wife, which faced each other across the curved stairway.

Behind her, Laura heard a thump, as one of their bags smacked against the floor. She turned to check that neither bag had come open, flinging its contents across the brightly-polished parquet floor.

"Where did Felix go?" she asked, smiling encouragingly at

the sweating Harvey, still struggling to manage his load.

Harvey's sunny smile widened and he pointed to the far end of the entry hall. The door stood half-open, and Laura could see Felix sitting at a small antique desk. He spoke urgently into the phone then paused to listen attentively, with his head cocked to one side.

"Very important," Harvey panted. "Felix says it's *very* important. He's afraid someone's going to put up skyscrapers across the canyon—or something." He smiled, as if he had made a very funny joke.

"You'd better not let Felix hear you making fun of him about of that," Laura said sympathetically. "I don't imagine he'd be too happy about it."

"I'd get my head handed to me, that's what!" Harvey clapped a hand over his mouth and giggled silently, rocking back and forth on his heels.

Laura didn't know whether or not it was fear she felt at the sight of a grown man carrying on like a child, but she could not make herself keep looking. She turned toward the mirror, busying herself with a few slight repairs to her makeup and blonde tresses. She was alert, though, for any disturbance from the study where Felix was telephoning.

"If you can tell me what room I'll be staying in, Harvey, I could go on up and get settled...."

"Staying? Oh yes, Mother mentioned that you'd be staying here."

"My name is Laura—Laura Foster, Harvey. I'm very pleased to meet you." She held out her cool dry hand to him. He wiped his sweaty palm on the side of his pants and tentatively followed suit.

"Mother told me that, too," Harvey said. He seemed very pleased at this example of his mother's planning and foresight. "She told me that a 'Miss Laura Foster' would be here, for just a little while, and she said she herself, Mother that is, would make all the arrangements."

"So where is your mother, then?"

"Ah, well that's the whole point, isn't it?" Harvey bent toward Laura and stage-whispered: "She's gone!"

"But did she tell you which room I'm to stay in before she left?"

"Nope. Not a word," Harvey said regretfully. "But Mother doesn't like you, I'm afraid," he added unnecessarily.

From a short distance away, over the noise of Harvey's heavy feet shuffling awkwardly along the hardwood floor and of Felix dialing yet another phone number in the adjacent room, Laura heard what sounded like the tap-tap of a cane striking the floor in what could only be repressed fury.

"So your mother has left the house?" Laura said patiently. "Didn't she even want to stay long enough to meet me?"

"Well, she—she *had* to go."

"And of course she couldn't possibly be in the next room— listening to you tell me all this right now. Am I right?"

"She told me to *tell* you she was gone." Harvey's voice soared with the discomfort of the lie. "I think she'll pick out a room for you, later on—when she comes back."

"In that case, I guess I'll just change my clothes right here in the hall," Laura said. "If it were not for my wanting to look nice and make Felix glad he brought me here, I would never dream of changing my clothes right here and now—out in the hallway, I mean."

Harvey's eyes bulged. "Oh, no! You mustn't! You can't do that!"

They were interrupted almost immediately. First, in the library, Felix slammed the receiver down against its cradle; then, to Laura's right, from in back of a closed double door, the tip of a cane struck hard at the floor.

One of the double doors opened on a flinty-eyed woman in her mid-fifties. The resemblance to Felix, except for the curled gray hair and the fine spider web of lines around her eyes, was uncanny.

"So," she said, in a voice nearly as deep as Felix's. "You've caused quite enough trouble in this house already, young woman."

"I have no idea what you're talking about...," Laura said, in genuine confusion.

"Indeed. Then come into this room and see for yourself."

Selina Page didn't bother to gesture or hold the door open, but turned around and walked away. Laura, her brows knitted in perplexity, followed.

Laura found herself in the sort of room that could only be described as a salon. The furniture was French baroque; the mirrors were Chippendale with fine gold scrollwork around them. The walls were upholstered in green velvet. Laura immediately recognized a Degas and a Monet, and not for a moment did she doubt that they were originals.

The surface of the gilt cocktail table in the middle of the room was almost covered with several large bunches of lilacs in cellophane, and two more floral packages had been laid, unopened, on the floor beneath. Selina pointed in disgust at the flowers.

"I mean those—*flowers*!" she snapped. "They've been arriving all day—and I won't stand for it any longer!"

"I suppose they were sent by my friend Rochelle and some of the people I work with," Laura said. "I'm sure they're intended for Felix as much as for me."

"Well, it makes no difference who sent them. They have to be thrown out," Selina said briskly, in a tone intended to close all argument. "I won't have them in my house."

"Those flowers were sent to me by people I know," Laura, replied, choosing her words with care, "and I intend to keep them for as long as I possibly can."

"We'll see about that."

There was a green-fringed bell pull to one side of the lavish fireplace. Selina, cane fixed firmly in her left hand, advanced toward it to signal for a servant.

Felix, just having entered, broke in. "What's wrong? What's going on with you two?"

He stood in the opened door as stiffly as a soldier on parade. There was a thin, angry line on each side of his cheeks, probably from the nature of the phone conversations he'd been having.

"Nothing's 'going on.' Nothing at all," Selina said, tugging sharply at the bell pull before she turned to smile at her son. "Just a little misunderstanding, dear, but I'll set everything straight. Did you have a good trip down?"

"Fair," he said quickly, and gave her one of his patented engaging smiles. "But I've brought Laura with me, and that alone makes up for any trouble I may have been having lately. I'm sure that the two of you are going to get along just fine."

Taking in Felix's boyish grin, Laura was suddenly able to understand how a person might be driven to violence out of pure frustration.

"*Your* young friend here," Selina said, with a toss of her gray curls in Laura's direction, "has taken it upon herself to have all these *things* delivered—before she even arrived here. Obviously Miss—ah, Foster—seems to be a very popular young lady—in some circles."

Felix turned to Laura, hesitating to ask the question that was obviously on his mind.

"Well, it looks as if your mother and I have gotten off on the wrong foot," Laura said as evenly as she could. "I'll just take the flowers to my room, and that ought to solve the problem."

"I've got an allergy to flowers." Selina interjected, her mouth hard and her eyes narrowed to a steely glint. She didn't look as if she'd ever known a moment's weakness in her entire life. "The doctor told me so just recently, and I know I just wouldn't be able to breathe—if there were any flowers in this house."

The thin, angry red lines of Felix's cheeks suddenly pulsed and glowed again.

Behind him, a woman's quiet voice asked deferentially, "Did somebody ring?"

Felix stepped into the salon and to one side. A maid took his place in the doorway. She appeared to be in her mid-forties, and looked attentive and very much at ease.

"I did, Susan," Selina said, and gestured toward the cocktail table. "Take those bouquets out of here. You can give them to a sick friend of yours, or to some charity, if you'd prefer."

Selina glanced at Laura with an air of satisfaction. One tight gray curl suddenly dropped across Selina's right eye as her head was popped back in surprise.

For Laura had walked confidently over to the cocktail table and picked up the larger of the two bunches of cellophane-wrapped lilacs.

"I'll just take these upstairs to my room," she said, turning her back on the shocked Selina, who tap-tapped her cane on the floor some half a dozen times before she could think of a response to this treason.

"I want you to know there have been members of the Page family living in this house since the Civil War." She glared at Laura's rigid back, "and we aren't accustomed to being contradicted in our own home by some *stranger* who happens to be visiting."

Laura, her nerves as taut as violin strings, made a point of turning around politely and smiling, before saying: "Why, Selina. I suspect we'll get to know each other so well that I can't be considered a stranger at all."

Laura had one satisfying glimpse of Selina's face whitening with anger as she understood the implication behind Laura's words. She looked at her son in disbelief, as if asking herself whether he would insist on marrying this creature against her own wishes. She glared back at Laura who added:

"Please ask your maid to show me to my room so that I can take a nap and freshen up before dinner."

Laura didn't complain about the distant room with the incongruous round bed in the wing furthest from the main part of the house; she vowed not to cause any more trouble, if possible, for Felix's sake. She was just settling down for a brief nap, when there was a soft tap at the door. Laura drew on her robe and asked who was there.

"Me," Felix answered softly. "May I talk to you for a couple of minutes?"

He sat on the one chair in the room and looked admiringly at

Laura for a minute or so then he told her what was on his mind. He wanted to apologize for his mother's bad manners.

"As you've no doubt noticed, she's used to having her own way," he explained, "and the gout that requires her use of a cane doesn't help her disposition either."

"I'm sure your mother and I will get used to each other in time," Laura said soothingly. "I'm just tired from the trip, and I'm sure she's a little apprehensive with someone new in the house. Don't worry about it, Felix. And please don't let yourself get overly upset by all this."

"Mother always thought that the only girl I should show a serious interest in would be one of the local girls from a good family. Mother even had picked out a girl, then couldn't understand why I hesitated."

"She'll get over her disappointment, I'm sure."

"You certainly declared 'war' downstairs when you took those flowers away from her." He smiled ruefully. "I guess Mother enjoys a good fight now and then. But she may have a lot more on her hands in a few months than even she can handle."

"Whatever do you mean?"

"The developers really *are* closing in on El Norte, Laura, with a vengeance."

Felix was tight-lipped now. He stood up and began pacing the room to work off additional energy.

"Are you sure?"

"Yes, of course I am. This isn't the vacation season yet, for example, but we're still getting close to eight thousand cars a day clogging the local roads. Last summer, in fact, El Norte State Park turned away hundreds of people every week because there were no camping facilities to take care of all of them."

"But what does that have to do with the motel owners and people like that?"

"When the tourists come, the leeches won't be far behind," Felix said, throwing the words over a shoulder as he paced the room. "Why do you suppose plans are being made to widen the highway? So that more cars can come in. Oh, the developers are on to El Norte, all right; make no mistake about that."

"You can't just keep people out—not if they want to come here," Laura began reasonably.

"We're not trying to," Felix pointed out with more patience than she might have expected. "Our best hope is to keep El Norte from becoming part of the grand motel complex, to keep just a little beauty left untouched in this world, a little place where people can go and feel closer to—well, to God. This *is* a crusade on my part, Laura: nothing less than a crusade. I hope you understand that."

"But what do you plan to do about it?"

"First of all, I'm going to attend a meeting tonight—of local property owners—and I hope you'll come with me. Then maybe we can bring others in on our plans to save El Norte. I don't want to discover, when it's too late, that somebody is putting up a gas station or a fast food joint right across the road from Coralton."

"Coralton?"

"This property. Didn't I tell you that the name of this house is Coralton? No, I suppose I didn't. So many things have been happening that you can't blame me for not having remembered to tell you such a simple thing as that."

"Felix, I don't think I could ever blame you for anything," she said quietly.

He didn't seem to hear the suppressed affection in her voice; he couldn't pull his mind away from what was, to him, the biggest problem of all.

"I hope you don't think that everybody in El Norte is on my side, Laura. Rich people live around here, you know, and if there's more money to be had by selling out to the developers, a lot of them will want to go for it. The rich live in a very simple world of black and white, you know, when everything is said and done."

"You'll persuade them to do what's right," Laura said calmly. "I know you will."

"I don't know. I sometimes get too excited in the midst of an argument and lose my self-control." He set his jaw tightly. "I just wish that somebody who's better at persuasion than I am would take care of that side of it. I know I'd feel a lot happier if I didn't have to go around arguing with my neighbors."

"Are you absolutely certain, Felix, that the overall situation is as bad as you think it is?"

"If anything, it's probably worse," he said gravely, then gave an apologetic little smile and continued. "That phone call I made—I found out that the Highway Commission is set to revamp El Norte completely, cutting out what it calls 'danger spots'— They'll nibble away at more and more of the land until there'll be nothing left at all. Well, it's not going to happen, not if I can help it. I'll fight my neighbors, the State Commission, and the whole world, if I have to, Laura, but the developers aren't going to get their dirty hands on El Norte. I don't care what I have to do to make sure El Norte stays like it is; but that's what I'll do."

His fists opened partway and formed a rough circle, as if he were getting ready to wring somebody's neck in vicious anger. But he suddenly whirled around and left the room, slamming the door behind him. At first, his steps sounded like a rapid tattoo of drumbeats along the hall, reminiscent of his mother's tap-tapping with the cane, but they became softer in a little while, and then there were longer intervals between succeeding steps, until finally they couldn't be heard any more.

Laura hoped that the tension in him would be dissipated for now and that their dinner would go smoothly. As concerned as she was, her exhaustion took over and, in a short time, Laura drifted off into a sound sleep.

In her dream, she was the center of all eyes at her fabulous coming-out party, except that her wealthy parents continued to quarrel between themselves. Her father, a sharp-featured man who reminded her of Felix, forgot to dance the first dance with her. When Laura reminded him, he grew angry; he yanked her to the floor and grabbed her hard around the waist. The pressure on her grew heavier. She was losing her balance now, and her eyes swayed from one gaudy dress to another; the jarring music assaulted her ears. Suddenly an admiring pair of eyes, very close to hers, seemed to be jabbing into her psyche as sharply as the hand gripping her waist. What was this man doing to her? she wondered. Wasn't he her father? Wasn't it true that she'd always lived with her real parents, instead of spending her childhood in one strange house after another? Hadn't she *always* known security, warmth, and the happiness of being loved and cheri....

Abruptly she awoke to discover that she was crying—bitterly and inconsolably—and couldn't quite remember why

CHAPTER FOUR

Laura was feeling rested and more at ease when she walked back into the salon just before dinner. The jungle of French baroque now seemed at least reasonably familiar to her, and she could tell it had been in place for a very long time. Permanence lent charm even to garishness, at least in Laura's unsophisticated eyes.

Selina Page had been standing like a sentinel near the middle of the room, blocking out the cocktail table and chairs near it. She wore a white and navy blue dress, in a style popular perhaps ten years before, as if she had no need to care about current styles. The strands of her silver-gray hair gleamed silkily in the light from the fireplace. Felix entered the room shortly after Laura and Selina smiled fondly at him. She took a firm grip on the handle of her cane and stepped to her right.

"Look! Look who's here, Felix!" she said triumphantly, gesturing with her free hand toward the gathered chairs. "Aren't you happy to see her?"

"How are you, Felix?" the newcomer's soft, husky voice purred. "I haven't seen you since...in such a long time. I hope your visit to New York was pleasant and profitable?"

"Yes, it was. *Very* pleasant." Felix said, recovering his composure. "I'd like you to meet Laura Foster. This is Janice Ulric, Laura. She's one of our neighbors."

"More than that, I hope," Janice twinkled back at Felix. "How do you do, Miss Foster," Janice said coolly to Laura and turned back eagerly to Felix. "I hope your nerves are better by now."

"They had been," Felix said, "until I heard about the Highway Commission's plans to destroy El Norte."

"And now you feel like dropping somebody from a high place, I suppose," Janice said as if referring to an amusing quirk of character. "You were *always* so impulsive, Felix."

She glanced directly at Laura, and the true meaning of her remark became clear: Bringing an "outsider" to Coralton could be considered an impulsive act.

Laura returned the glance appraisingly. Janice was much taller than Laura, and probably a bit older. Her hair was red and lustrous, her green eyes sparkled, her skin was soft and glowing, and her figure had been developed with loving and expensive care. Wealth had lent her a poise which wasn't far short of arrogance.

Felix also had caught the nuanced meaning in the redhead's comment. "I'm not *that* impulsive, Janice. I just always seem to know exactly what I want—and don't want."

He then made a point of smiling warmly at Laura—and she smiled just as warmly back at him. Janice sat back as if she couldn't quite believe that Felix actually preferred someone like Laura to a wealthy beauty such as herself.

"But the point is, dear Felix," Janice murmured, "for you to decide whether what you *want* is really *right* for you."

The pulse in Felix's left temple was hammering furiously. Laura folded a hand into his and felt him hold her tightly at first and then more loosely as he regained his composure.

The door was suddenly flung open and Harvey made a grand entrance. He had dressed too quickly for dinner, and one of the little buttons at the top of his collar had come undone, sending it flopping to one side. The blank smile that he turned on the assembled group might have been engraved on his thick, fleshy lips.

"Hello Felix, hello, uh, Miss Foster, hello Mother, and—why, hello Janice. Long time no see."

"Thank you. Harvey," Janice said coldly, annoyed that the wrong man had welcomed her with such enthusiasm.

Selina was no longer interested in the small talk. "Now that we're all here," she said, "we can go in to dinner. Felix, will you take *our guest*"—indicating Janice—"into the dining room?"

"I invited Janice to have dinner with us tonight," Selina went on, once they were all seated at the lovely old refectory table in the dining room, "because I think it's high time that you, my sweet"—she turned again to Janice—"and Felix, my dear, started to make your plans for the future."

Felix, sitting beside Janice, where his mother had placed him, pointedly turned to say something to his half-brother on the other side, steadfastly ignoring his mother's remarks.

Harvey also behaved as if nothing disturbing was happening. "I'm sure Janice will have a very good future." He smiled crookedly. "Well, any member of the Ulric family—a female, I mean—can expect marriage and children and everything that goes with it."

"A good marriage is exactly what I want to talk about," Selina went on firmly. "I realize that it may seem premature, but the matter is far too important to put off any longer. It's been understood for years that Janice and Felix would marry, and I think it's high time that the two of you began to make arrangements for going through with it."

Laura, listening to the strong-minded older woman, knew that Felix was being forced into an untenable position where he'd be forced to fight against his mother's will—if he were to have a say in his own future. He sat glaring at his mother in silence. In back of him, and at his right against the wall, a Vermeer painting showed a sweet-faced nun, who appeared to be looking over the troubling scene with a perplexed smile on her cherubic face.

Finally, Felix said, "I don't want to go into it."

"Excuse me, Felix dear? What did you say?" his mother said.

"I said: I don't want to discuss it now."

"Felix, both of you put matters off a few months ago when you left El Norte. Now it's time to begin making plans."

Janice broke in. "There was no choice when we had to delay

our marriage before, but I don't see why we can't talk about the situation now. This is as good a time and place as any."

"Are you both out of your minds?" Felix's voice was rising. "Laura is right here, and *she's* the one I've made up my mind to—"

Selina interrupted briskly. "Now don't say anything you'll be sorry for later, Felix dear."

Harvey, with a smile, turned to Laura and said pleasantly, "You know, it's really amazing to me that someone like Janice would still want to marry into the Page family, considering how much she knows about us, I mean."

Selina interrupted him, "Whatever you're about to say, Harvey, is not important. Stop it this instant."

"I was just going to say that the Pages are a difficult family," Harvey persisted. "Well, we all know that. After all, Felix has a *very* bad temper that tends to get him into trouble, and me? I guess I'm probably El Norte's idea of the village idiot!" He chortled at the idea. "For Janice to marry in to this mess takes guts. Or, if you prefer a nicer phrase, intestinal fortitude."

At any other time, Laura would have taken a small amount of pleasure in watching Selina's response. She made such a violent motion in Harvey's direction that she nearly swept her half-empty soup bowl off the table.

"Harvey, stop this nonsense immediately!" she demanded.

"But I'm serious about this," Harvey said, although the crooked smile never left his lips. "My hat is off to you, Janice, for being willing to accept a brother-in-law who's never held a job and who will *never* ride in an automobile—since that terrible accident nearly fifteen years ago—well, I spent seven months in the hospital afterwards, and I still have to take .treatments, occasionally, so it's understandable. You know, it's fortunate I've got those two incomes: the one from my real father's estate, and the supplement from Mother's second husband, Mr. Page. He adopted me, you know," he added, turning to Laura. "And I took the name of Page. As I say, Janice knows she'd be letting herself in for some tricky social situations, yet she's still willing to marry into the tribe; and my hat's off to her because of it." He sat back in his chair, exhausted by the effort of his presentation.

"Leave this table, Harvey," Selina shouted, all dignity gone at last. "Leave this table at once!"

Harvey looked satisfied, but slightly worn, as if he had accomplished a great chore. He rose from his chair slowly, nodded cordially at Laura, and made his good-byes politely to the others, as if he were leaving the table of his own accord. He tried to shake Janice's hand, apparently to express his sincere admiration for her, but the haughty young woman turned away from him—as if he didn't exist. Harvey saluted his mother cheerfully and walked out, whistling under his breath.

"I hope that the two of you will agree on a June wedding," Selina continued as if nothing had happened. "But you've postponed it so long now that perhaps you'd rather do something earlier than that. Spring is nice...."

Ignoring her completely, Felix turned instead to Laura. "You know, Laura, I do like Janice, just because I more or less grew up with her. But I do *not* want to marry her."

"I think I deserve the courtesy of being spoken to directly, Felix," Selina said. "I suppose you're under the spell of this young woman. But once you've thought about it some—the propriety, I mean—I have no doubt you will change—"

"My feelings are not going to change, Mother," he snapped. "I'm not the same man I was when I left here a few months ago, and whatever feelings I might have thought I had at the time have changed. I'm very sorry, but I'm afraid you've asked Janice here under false pretenses."

Selina, by habit, tap-tapped on the refectory table with the crook of her cane. "I'll overlook that outburst, as I've done so often in the past," she said slowly. "Mother love often requires overlooking or ignoring ingratitude from your offspring."

"My mind is made up," Felix responded. "Ingratitude or not, I will not marry Janice."

Janice had sat nearly motionless since Harvey's somewhat eerie discussion of the Page family problems and of his own mental imperfections. Now she turned to Felix and smiled thinly.

"I suppose you've actually decided to marry this—this 'fortune hunter,'" she said, as if she was referring to someone who wasn't in the same room with them, "because she has flattered your ego. And I'm sure it'll all work out just fine—if the girl can get used to your wretched temper—and if you tell her the truth about yourself before she says 'I do.' If you tell her the *whole* truth about yourself, that is."

Felix winced. Laura promptly stood up and circled the table on her way out the door. Felix was at her side before she had taken a dozen steps. As they left the room they could hear Janice's voice following them:

"You should be as honest as Harvey was just now—and admit to Laura that you were forced to leave El Norte—"

"Don't listen to her. Just keep walking," Felix whispered.

"—because you murdered a man with your bare hands!" Janice finished loudly.

Laura's steps thankfully didn't falter, and Felix remained at her side, supporting with one arm.

"And if you can murder one human being," Janice added just before the door was closed on her, "you just possibly—for all I know—might—"

Laura's heart was pounding so loudly that she couldn't hear her own footsteps. And when she tried to look down she couldn't see what lay ahead of her.

Vaguely she was aware of Felix leading her, not upstairs to her bedroom, but to the front door and outside into the gathering gloom. Then he carefully helped her into a car with plush seats so wide and deep that her feet, on such a petite frame, couldn't quite touch the carpeted floor when she sat back in relief. Felix started the car, swerved around the brick-paved drive and out toward the street. When Laura looked back at the towering old mansion, where the two women she had just met had unleashed hostile tongues against her, she was afraid she would be able to feel no more at home at Coralton than she had at any one of the numerous foster homes she had known in the past.

As the car reached that part of the highway known as Florida 3, a myriad of stars winked and glittered at her through the spotless windshield.

"I know you must want to know what in the world Janice was talking about," Felix said between clenched teeth. He sat with his head almost between his shoulders, with his strong, hard hands holding tightly to the dark-brown steering wheel.

"I haven't asked you about it, have I?"

"It would be a relief to get it off my chest. Believe it or not, Laura, I meant to tell you the whole business before I—well, I certainly don't want to talk about *that*, right now. At some other time, yes, but not until you know all about this other thing."

Laura didn't know how to comfort him, and in the lengthening silence between them, she listened to the mesmerizing purr of the tires and the steely chuckle of the car's exhaust.

"Actually it's why I was so secretive about myself back in New York," he finally admitted. "And I certainly didn't want to be seen by anybody who might have known something about my 'problem.' That's why I was so sure that your friend, Rochelle, had recognized me; I knew that my picture had appeared in newspapers outside of Florida after this hellish thing happened. It's been the hardest thing of all for me to keep hiding the story from you, Laura. But I didn't know how to tell you—"

"And you're still hiding it," she said accusingly. "I haven't the slightest idea what you're talking about...."

"I know I'm talking *around* what happened, Laura, instead of talking *about* it. It's simple enough, though, and I can say it all in less than a minute, as soon as I get my nerve up."

His face was red and his voice had risen. But there didn't seem to be any anger left in him, only a dread of getting out the next word—and the one after that.

"Mother, as you have probably realized, found herself with two young boys to raise after the death of her second husband, my father. If she needed advice from a man, she never asked for it. In fact, she pretty well kept to herself, making decisions and forcing me and Harvey to carry them out as we grew older. My late father's business partner, Eldon Butterworth, had offered to do what he could, but Mother turned his help down each and every time. That is, Laura, until Harvey had his car accident. Then she realized that this was a crisis she couldn't handle on her own, just by telling us what to do and putting enough pressure on until we did it."

"Selina sounds..." Laura hesitated, "...fearsome."

"She can be, yes." Felix stared straight ahead of him at the road. "She ended up going to Eldon for advice after all. He was an astute businessman who owned valuable property in El Norte, not too far from Coralton. They had known each other for many years, and he had never married. They seemed, at first, to have a great deal in common, and with her growing dependence on him, he got it into his head that they should marry."

Laura nodded. "It must have been nice for her to have known the same person for years and years—someone who could help shoulder the burden...."

"But she decided Eldon was too cantankerous and set in his ways for marriage," Felix went on carefully. "She'd lost two husbands already and wasn't going to risk losing a third. In fact, she decided she didn't *want* a third husband. And when my mother makes up her mind to something, it nearly always happens that way."

"I'm not surprised," Laura murmured.

A house suddenly loomed up in front of them in the headlights, a modern glass-walled affair with a sprawling garage standing open to several vehicles parked inside.

"But what happened to Mr. Butterworth?" Laura asked.

"There isn't much to tell," Felix said, slowing the car. "He and my mother remained close friends, and Harvey and I were taught to call him 'Uncle' Eldon. He was, in many ways, a father figure, and a valuable part of our lives. But I saw less and less of him as I went away to school each year; and when I came back for the holidays or on breaks, I began to see him in a different light. Instead of a generous Santa Claus, he began to seem greedy and acquisitive to me, like some kind of Scrooge."

"Businessmen have a great regard for money, or so I've been told," Laura said wryly.

"But you've never seen someone like this up close and personal, Laura, and you can still keep your illusions about them. Uncle Eldon was typical of the breed as it really is. He talked about free enterprise as though such a thing really existed, and as if he wasn't ready and willing to cut the throat of any real business competition—or, on the other hand, join with them to fix prices illegally. He also talked a lot about the government's interference with free enterprise, never realizing that he couldn't make even a reasonably good living unless the government regulated standards and remained one of his biggest customers. I once told him that, and I said that *he* was growing fat and sassy under socialism; but his sixty-dollar-a-week clerks in the 'right-to-work' states, the men and women who'd be fired if they joined a union—*those* people were living under the 'glories' of the free enterprise system. I told him that if socialism is good enough for the rich, then that's the way everybody in this country ought to be living."

Laura smiled slightly. "It sounds as if you'd picked up some of those ideas at college."

"Oh, sure, I was quoting some of my political science professors, all right," Felix admitted. "But I'll be damned if Eldon didn't jump six feet in the air and accuse me a being a Communist *and* worst of all, a Democrat, just as if the two were the same thing! At any rate, you can see how his mind worked, and you can see how he would have reacted to the suggestion that part of El Norte ought to be used for setting up cheap motels at fifty-mile intervals."

"You mean he was in favor of it."

"Of course he was. 'El Norte,' he said, 'is only a place to live; and there are plenty of others to choose from if you feel that privacy is so necessary. You've got to move with the times,' Eldon said to us at dinner one evening. And did we have any idea how much more valuable our properties would become if there were a real red-hot tourist rush? If we were to sell out just before the rush came to a peak, why, we'd clean up a small fortune."

Laura was beginning to understand what had happened between Felix and his late father's business partner.

"I take it for granted that you got angry at him then."

"Of course I did! I felt as if I'd been betrayed, by one of my own, so to speak. You know, Laura, there are still a few class-conscious snobs left in society who expect a certain code of standards to be followed by our own class. I suppose I'm making a hash out of explaining this, Laura, but I really know what I mean—if that's any consolation."

"Probably you do." Laura didn't want to speculate about class-conscious snobs; the immediate image rising to her brain was that of Selina Page ordering her to leave Coralton forever. "And I suspect that you rushed at Eldon Butterworth and hit him," she went on.

Felix said impassively, "I put my hands around his neck and tried to strangle him."

He made a right turn and he and Laura were suddenly sitting inside the garage. After he was parked—Felix remained sitting in the driver's seat and looked down at his ten fingers spread out before him on the steering wheel, as if they were had betrayed him....

"And *did* you choke him to death?" Laura asked, surprised at how calm she felt.

"I tried my best, Laura, believe me, I tried. Of course this happened at the dinner table, as I said, and my whole family moved to stop me. Harvey did his best to pull me off Eldon. But it was no use; it was not the time for appealing to my finer feelings, I'm afraid. I pushed Harvey away from me, and that brought Mother directly into the fray."

"Your mother didn't try to soothe you down, I take it."

"No, she just kept hitting me with her cane until I finally gave up and turned away. Eldon sat down, gasping. I swear his face was completely blue. My mother phoned a doctor, but Eldon got it into his head to go home before the doctor could get there; he didn't want to spend another second under the same roof with me. And, in a way, I don't suppose I really blamed him."

"But what happened to Eldon?"

"He had left the house by the time the doctor arrived and Mother went with him to Eldon's house. She stayed there until Eldon had been thoroughly examined and was resting comfortably. The doctor said that Eldon had been badly shaken up, but that, in his opinion, there was nothing really wrong with him. I assume that, from the whispers between Eldon and my mother, the doctor was able to figure out who was responsible for what had happened to Eldon."

"But he wouldn't need to make it public unless there was a police investigation."

"There *was* one. During the night Eldon's heart acted up— and in the morning, he was dead. At the inquest, I was put under the spotlight. No legal action was taken against me, but Mother insisted that it would be better if I spent a few months out of the state. The job offer in New York came along just then, and I took it. It turned out pretty well after all, Laura, considering that I met you there." He turned to her expectantly.

Laura said nothing.

"I don't suppose, after hearing all this, that you'd want to—I mean, that you'd want anything to do with me. You probably think I might even hurt *you*."

Laura suddenly reached over and took both his clenched hands in hers. Then she drew them to the sides of her neck and pressed—hard.

Felix pulled his hands away from her neck and touched her hair. He looked down at her with wonder.

"I promise you'd never regret—" he began.

Just then a horn blared behind them in the garage. Felix turned away from Laura and quickly checked the rearview mirror. Another car slipped in behind, the driver waving at them with cheerful encouragement, puckering his lips to indicate that Felix ought to go ahead and kiss his girl friend. Then he threw back his head and laughed.

"What a jerk! With idiots like him on the committee we might just as well forget about El N—" Felix stopped himself. "No, I'm not giving up, Laura. Come on. Let's go see if we can change some minds."

CHAPTER FIVE

Felix entered the glass-walled house with all the ease and familiarity of one who once had lived there. He told Laura afterwards that he knew this house—and most of the others in El Norte for that matter—only a little less well than he knew Coralton.

They entered through a long, gallery-style hall with starkly white walls lavishly adorned with brightly-colored artwork in the modern style. An opened baby grand piano commanded one end of the room they entered, and an Eames-style table and three-legged chair stood at attention, like pieces of sculpture, at the other. Two large sectional sofas, all upholstered in a strong tropical print, were arranged to form a conversation area. Bright throw pillows and throws had been placed here and there.

A large, attractive man, obviously the owner of the house, stood drink in hand, casually dressed in a Hawaiian sports shirt, casual slacks, and sandals. He was the center of a rapt audience of half-a-dozen, and seemed to be discussing reproduction rights and the legalized robbery practiced by gallery owners in New York. Felix approached and introduced him to Laura as the contemporary artist Ned Boyer. She timidly began to ask him about a series of abstract paintings she thought he'd done, but he turned away from her and began talking with his cronies once again about business details and legal technicalities.

One of the men in the group was older and was more conservatively dressed all in black set off by a crisp white shirt. His hair was gray at the temples, and he stood at attention like a soldier on parade.

He nodded distantly at Felix, but the glare he sent Laura's way seemed to her to be filled with quiet loathing.

Felix drew a taut breath and Laura looked over at him in apprehension. She had no idea what she had done to draw the stranger's obvious dislike.

"What's the matter, Gordon?" Felix asked. "Are you still sore at me because of Janice?"

"I have no intention of talking to you about my daughter, or anything else for that matter." Gordon Ulric said.

"Not in the least. But I don't want you giving Miss Foster here a bad time because of it. None of this has anything to do with her."

"If we have to talk about this, we can do it some other time, in private." Gordon Ulric made as if to turn away from Felix.

"All the same, I hope we understand each other, Gordon."

"Are you at each other's throats already? This is shaping up to be an interesting meeting." Another voice had chimed in cheerfully and all three turned at once to see who it was.

The newcomer stood framed in the entrance to the room, just beneath a steel catwalk which spanned the area above, joining two of the bedroom wings of the house. It was the horn-blower who had driven into the garage just as Felix had been about to kiss Laura, and he was no more welcome at this moment than he had been then, as far as Felix was concerned.

The man was probably in his late forties, tall and ruddy-faced. He blinked rapidly and continuously, a dead giveaway that he was wearing new contact lenses. His teeth gleamed brightly, almost blindingly, and his ready smile evoked a cheerful demeanor.

"I don't believe I've made your acquaintance," he said, holding out his hand to Felix, "but you've got good taste in women." His eyes slid appreciatively over Laura's petite form. "My name is Clymer, Oscar Clymer. I've just purchased the Butterworth estate, a few gopher holes away."

"Felix Page here," Felix said, shaking the proffered hand

Laura heard a sudden *pop-popping* sound just after their hands made contact, a sound that reminded her of an alarm going off. Felix withdrew his hand hurriedly and looked down at his palm. Oscar Clymer threw back his head and laughed heartily, just as he'd done when he caught them in the garage.

"The old reliable joke always works the best," Clymer crowed. He raised one hand as if he were a policeman stopping traffic.

"Now before you get around to calling me all sorts of names, Mr. Page, I should tell you that I am the founder and CEO of the E-Z Joke Corporation. I manufacture and market what are called practical jokes and gags. Now Mr. Ulric here is a banker and he thinks about debentures; our host, Ned Boyer, is an *artiste*, and all he thinks about *chiarascuros*. But me? I'm in the practical joke business and I try out things like these joy buzzers on unsuspecting people. My heart is in my work, you know. I'm a dedicated man."

Clymer, a thoughtful frown on his face, chuckled, then suddenly made certain noises suggestive of an Indian. Then he muttered to himself, "No, I might lose my shirt on it...." He turned to Gordon Ulric. "What do you think, Gordie? About a rubber tomahawk, I mean. Would *you* buy it for your grandson?"

"Frankly, Mr.—ah—"

"Clymer, but the first name is Oscar and not Social—you know, 'social climber'—get it? I was just thinking about this group as being 'all these chiefs and not enough Indians,' and that gave me this idea for a toy and I've even got a name for it and I think it will look good on a package. The name is 'Oomgowa!' It's got appeal and it'll make 'em laugh, so it ought to catch on. What do you think?"

Laura couldn't see how Gordon Ulric would manage to get away from Oscar Clymer's obtrusive cheerfulness, but when she looked again, the man was sitting at the Eames table, writing a memorandum to himself.

He continued, from time to time looking up and smiling at them all affably, then finally got up and moved to one of the tropical print sofas where he plunked down with a sigh of appreciation. "Well," he said, raising his voice and speaking to the room at large, "Are we all just going to sit here? Or shall we try to decide how we're going to keep all those undesirable elements out of our neighborhoods?"

The room had been filling up with new arrivals, and Felix seemed to know most of them. He greeted each one with genuine pleasure, asking how their lives had been proceeding in the last few months, and everybody he talked to seemed to Laura to be glad that Felix hadn't had any more problems over Eldon's death. Someone said to Felix that he didn't think he'd changed much since high school, and Laura couldn't help being a little envious of the friend who had known Felix for such a long time.

Ned Boyer finally raised his hand, calling for quiet. But before he could say anything, there was a sudden thudding sound that reminded Laura of the way a bomb sounds on television. Oscar Clymer studied the mixed reactions, the only person in the room who wasn't shocked by the noise. He got up and presented a round black ball with a cord at one end, to the host.

"The E-Z Bomb," he explained, pointing to a colophon just beneath the base of the cord. "Guaranteed to keep order at meetings, among other things. It has a hundred and one uses, none of them a bit important. Take this one with my compliments, Neddie, and use it in good health."

Ned Boyer smoothly avoided further discussion by holding the toy bomb to the side in one hand. He turned back to the group. "We all know why we're here, so let's begin. We need to talk about what we intend to do to meet the danger to our community head-on. Who'll start?— All right, Felix."

The group quieted down. Ned Boyer's wife, who was also dressed casually in a pants suit and sandals, began serving coffee to the group as Felix began to talk.

"We all know that the danger consists of the developers coming in one step at a time and taking bigger slices at every step," he concluded. "They're organized and militant; we haven't been, until I suggested our having this get-together. The question we have to decide is really a very simple one: how can we stop the developers?"

The silence that followed was broken by Oscar Clymer saying meditatively: "*Oomgowa!* Yes, that really sounds all right."

Gordon Elric stood to be recognized. "I'd hate to think about facing a lengthy court battle and drawn-out litigation. I feel certain that our chances are better if we stay quiet and reasonable and well-behaved about this...." He glanced at Felix.

Felix jumped up. "The more noise we make, the better for us and for every other community that's faced with the same damn probl—"

Ned Boyer, determined not to let this discussion become overheated if he could help it, broke in: "Gordon has the floor right now, Felix."

"In fact, it has suddenly occurred to me," Gordon went on, with a thin, unctuous smile, "that there may be less harm in the long run if we just let a few motels come in. It may save a lot of messy washing of dirty linen in public, and I don't see the harm it will do—if it's clearly understood at he outset that new construction of that type in El Norte will be of a limited nature."

As he finished, he glanced once more at Felix.

Another in the group waved a hand: "But they'll never let it go at that—not even if there's a contract involved. Once these people have got a foot in the door, they won't stop until they're all the way in and you're forced out!"

Laura thrust up her hand as well. Ned looked startled and went around the room twice to make sure that nobody else wanted the floor. He then reluctantly gestured at Laura.

"It seems to me, as an outsider, of course," Laura said, her low, well-modulated voice commanding the same attention she had sought on the stage, "that none of you should let your personal feuds interfere with the question at hand. Preserving the integrity of El Norte is much more important than settling any old grievances...."

She had been looking directly at Gordon Ulric as she spoke, and the banker flushed and turned away, feigning interest in a neighbor's whispered conversation.

"That's all I have to say," she added and retook her seat.

Felix's hand found hers, and he said quietly, "Bless you for that, Laura."

She smiled back at him and then looked down at her lap.

Next the newcomer, Oscar Clymer, was recognized by the chairman and said with a chuckle, "Why don't we just threaten these motel people with stink bombs in their lobbies if they go through with this? I can get you all the bombs you'll need, and between us, we can make those people's lives miserable."

Someone else chimed in brightly, "Look here, all of you! If progress is inevitable in El Norte, we should get up a syndicate and put in some motels of our own. After all, why shouldn't *we* be the ones to cash in while we can?"

During the pained silence that greeted this bombshell, Ned made a point of looking up at the ceiling as if consulting the heavens.

"That's actually been proposed already," he said patiently, "by me, as well as a few others. But the consensus of the group is that we put that off as a last ditch measure, an admission of defeat if you will. We're all committed here to take the position that the El Norte area can—and should—be left intact."

"Now I have a serious suggestion," Oscar Clymer said, waving his notebook as if it were the map to a gold mine. "There are too many of us here to work on this in an orderly fashion. I move instead that we appoint a smaller committee to research all this and report back to us at a later date, and meanwhile," the impish grin was back, "we as individuals can find out how much each of our properties are actually worth to the developers on the open market."

"As chairman," Ned said, "I want to go on record that I'm opposed to the idea of a separate committee. In my opinion, it will be used as an excuse to put off making a decision about what has got to be done. Instead, I suggest that one person be appointed to take the helm, someone who is responsible, as well as committed, to preserving El Norte."

Laura spoke from her seat: "Felix, then. He is the best person for the job because he cares the most about the outcome."

Gordon, his lips pursed, said, "I'm not sympathetic to this scheme because of—well, I have my reasons; so I'm hereby withdrawing from the group." He stood up to a shocked silence. "But before I go, let me point out to you all that the entire community of El Norte is liable to get a black eye if we appoint someone who will run roughshod over any and all opposition, even physically, if he feels driven to it."

He made a point of smiling politely and shaking hands with various ones around the room, then turned to leave, back straight and head erect. At the doorway, he thanked Ned's wife for their hospitality and pecked her lightly on the cheek.

Felix purposely waited until Gordon's footsteps had faded away. "I want to point out that making me a committee of one to report on methods for saving the situation has definite advantages for all of us. For one thing, I'm so upset about this business that I'll probably spend every waking moment on it. But as we all know, speed *is* important, and one man is likely to work faster than two or more, arguing back and forth about everything. Also, I'm an architect by profession and I've seen this kind of takeover of an area tried before by packs of developers; if anybody can figure how to beat them at their own game, I can."

Ned rubbed his chin thoughtfully, then sighed as he realized that the next man waiting to be recognized was, once more, the practical joke man, Oscar Clymer, who clutched his memo book tightly to one side as he spoke: "I've got to admit, folks, that I don't see one thing wrong with this idea of giving Felix here the job he's so anxious to have."

Felix nodded and mouthed a 'thank you.'

Clymer saluted with his left hand, then added thoughtfully, "But you must understand that I haven't lived in El Norte long enough to make friends or enemies, for that matter. I'm simply not as attached to the place as the rest of you are. It may sound to some of you like high treason, but if I had to sell my house tomorrow because somebody had put up a peanut stand in front of it, for instance, I wouldn't think I was in the middle of a Greek tragedy; I'd just go ahead and sell it, for the best price I could, and forget about it. At the end of the day, if there's some real advantage to getting out, then let's all do it as a unit."

"Thank you, Oscar. We'll take that on advisement," Ned said quickly, grateful that Clymer hadn't exploded yet another practical joke in the room. "Does any one else want to—Arnie?"

The next speaker, a lanky young man with a two-day growth of beard, stood up: "I approve of putting Felix to work...."

Felix nodded at the man.

"...But there must be a deadline for the first report, and I suggest we make it as brief a deadline as possible. Let me remind you of how much time we've already wasted. We all rememb—"

But Felix immediately interrupted him:

"Thanks Arnie, and thanks to all of you for suggesting me for this job. It's exactly what I've been hoping for." He whispered to Laura on the side: "That guy will talk forever, given half a chance."

Laura whispered back, as the crowd began to discuss the final decision in earnest, "You know, I genuinely enjoyed recommending you...."

"Yep, I could sense that you were getting a hoot out of it." He grinned at her.

"Could you, really?"

"Yes, Laura. It seems that we're very much attuned to each other."

"I know so."

"I've been thinking about that, Laura, and my notion is that we ought to be even more attuned to each other than we are already."

"How can we manage that?" Laura's heart began to beat wildly, though she remained outwardly calm.

"This is no place to talk about it at all, you know." They had left their seats and were edging toward the gallery leading to the front door.

"Felix! We aren't *talking* in the proper sense of the word. We're *whispering*!"

"I didn't intend to get into this subject right now, of all the times in the world. I don't know how in the world it happened."

Laura said slowly, "We can save this conversation for another time, if you'd prefer. Or for after we leave here."

"No, you don't understand. It's gone way too far already. I need to say this thing now, once and for all, and get it over with, Laura. I've got to put myself out of this misery."

"*Have* you been miserable, Felix?" Laura finally felt in control of the situation now—and happily so.

"For the last couple of weeks I've known that I was going to ask you—" he paused long enough to look down at her smiling lips and bright eyes. "You're a devil, you know, a real practicing devil. You should hang out your shingle and let the whole world know what you are."

"We've drifted a long way from talking about that special subject of yours, Felix, *whatever it is*."

"What do you mean, 'whatever' it is'? You know damn well what I've been talking about?"

"I suppose I do."

"Well, Laura, what about it?"

"I'm not trying to drive you crazy, Felix, but you really have to actually *say* it."

"You're a vain creature, Laura Foster."

"No, it's not like that. It's just that so much of my life up to now has been spent outside those simple occasions that a girl needs every once in awhile, those treasured moments to remember. But I don't suppose you can relate to a word I'm saying, Felix Page!"

"I think I can. It's not so different for a man...."

"It's a wonder I can convey anything at all, when we're standing here, forced to whisper like children in school."

"I'll write you a note instead, and you can sue me for breach of promise afterwards."

"Nobody in a court of law would believe you were serious,

bringing up a thing like this right now, Felix."

"It brought itself up."

"And you're just an innocent bystander, Felix? Do you expect any court to believe that?"

"It's just that the whole thing has been on my mind for such a long time, and on top of everything else, it's been unsettle—"

Ned, still trying to wrap up the meeting looked up and said, "Felix, we'd all be able to hear you and Laura a lot better if you wouldn't whisper so much."

"We were just discussing what a great meeting this has been, Ned, but we'd really better be going. Mother will probably be waiting up to hear how things went...."

"And you need to talk to me about that certain mystical subject," Laura said under her breath as they thanked the Boyers for their hospitality.

"Oh, heavens, I thought you'd forgotten all about that! Well, no, I don't really suppose you would."

"Forgotten about what?"

"Don't play Little Miss Innocence with me." His voice was pitched at what she could only think of as an affectionate growl. "You know we're talking about an—an arrangement for you and me."

"'Arrangement' is a peculiar word."

"A legalized arrangement is what I mean."

"I understand that the sort of thing you seem to have in mind, Felix, becomes legal after seven years. There's a common-law statute, if I'm not mistaken...."

"You're driving me out of my mind! If you keep on like this, I'll be a wreck in no time."

"Well, we can fix *that*, if it doesn't please you. I'll just say goodbye, Felix."

"No, wait." His hand held hers tightly. "You know how hard it is for me to say the words, Laura, but I really think we could—you know—work it out together."

"Yes, Felix," she agreed softly. "I think we could make it work."

"I'm difficult, you know," he said. "Very moody sometimes, and temperamental as all hell."

"I'd be able to get along with you."

"Sometimes I get so upset that I can't bring myself to say anything, and I hit out instead. I'm sure I'd never do that to you, Laura, but it has happened—with other people."

"I'll never say I haven't being warned," she said. Words she was to remember vividly in the near future.

"All right, then, here goes: Laura, will you marry me?"

"Yes, oh *yes*! Of course I will!"

"When? I mean how soon?"

"Tomorrow, if that's what you want."

"Let's make it on Sunday, Laura, and get it over with; I can't stand waiting."

"All right, then, Felix. Sunday."

"We'll have to invite people very quickly."

"There's nobody I'd especially want to invite."

He asked, "Is that on my account? Because of all the unpleasantness? You know I'm perfectly willing to—"

"You don't have to do anything you aren't comfortable doing, not even for a minute," Laura said. "I'd never ask that of you."

They had been standing close together in a quiet niche near the entry and making an effort to keep their conversation low and private. Ned suddenly raised his voice. "Won't you two please pay attention to what's going on here? I would think you, Felix, in particular would want to listen more carefully— because we've just taken a vote that is going to concern you."

"A vote?" Ned had finally gotten Felix's attention. "About me?"

"Yes. I think you'll be pleased to learn that we've appointed you as a committee of one to report back to the rest of us on the whole problem of what's involved in preserving El Norte." Ned spoke in crisp and business-like tones. "There's one angle to it, though, that you probably won't like a bit."

Felix waited" "Well?"

"We want that report in exactly one week from tonight,"

"One week?" Felix was shocked. "But I was just planning—" He turned to Laura.

She smiled. "It's all right. You have to take care of this business first."

He leaned over and whispered to her again, "Then do you mind if we invite these people to the wedding? We'll have a quiet ceremony at the house, and a few friends ought to be welcome. I'm sure you'll like all of them as much as I do when you get to know them better."

"Of course I will, Felix," she said. "Invite every one of your friends if you want to."

Felix cleared his throat. "There's one other unfinished piece of business," he began, blushing furiously as he stood up and gestured at Laura to stand next to him.

* * * * * * *

Never in her life had Laura spent a night and day even remotely like the rest of that Friday night and all of Saturday.

She and Felix went home and held hands and talked until morning. When Selina appeared for breakfast, Felix nerved himself to tell her the news. Selina tried to convince Felix to postpone the wedding, but he refused, in no uncertain terms. She said nothing further after that, and Laura told herself gratefully that the older woman was planning to help with the celebration.

But it soon became obvious that Selina planned to do absolutely nothing to help with the wedding plans, and Laura embarked on a day's work that would make her dizzy long before mid-afternoon. She crossed her fingers and ordered a ready-made gown from one of the local bridal shops (hoping the size was true and it would actually fit her tiny figure) and arranged for catering services, including cake and champagne. The caterer took it upon himself to contact the El Norte newspaper, and a photographer was dispatched to take pictures of the happy couple for an announcement. Laura tried to refuse, knowing Felix would object, but the argument was cut short when Harvey wandered in and said cheerfully that he would pose for the picture instead. The photographer sighed, shrugged, and left in disappointment. Harvey remained as giddy as a child during all the activity, and he went into transports of happiness when Felix asked him to serve as best man.

Saturday rehearsals for the wedding were complicated by Selina's refusal to take part. Laura memorized her future mother-in-law's part as well as her own, confident that the older woman would change her mind about participating when the wedding actually began.

Later she found Selina moping by herself in the salon and started explaining to her about her part in the ceremony, but Selina shouted, "Stop!" When Laura looked at her in confusion, she got up and tap-tapped her way to the door.

The library phone rang as she was on her way out. Felix, who had been drawing up part of his preliminary report on ways of keeping El Norte intact, answered it. He spoke briefly, then said something in a loud voice, and replaced the phone with a furious clatter.

Laura eased past Selina and ran out of the door and into the library. It was a large room, and the hundreds of books lined on variously-sized shelves lent it an old-world aura. Felix was shaking his fist at the telephone.

"What happened, dear?" she asked cautiously.

"That was that moron!" he said finally, gasping for breath. "That *damned* idiot!"

Laura waited for him to calm down and tell her who he meant, rather than risk making him even angrier at her obtuseness.

"That was Clymer, the idiot with the practical jokes," Felix continued, clenching his fists. "If I had the nerve, I'd strangle him."

"What on earth did he want?"

"He wanted me to know that he is now part-owner of two parcels of land in El Norte and that he's decided to build on them—if he and his partner can get permission from the suburban development people."

"There's more to it than that, though, isn't there? You wouldn't care this much if we were talking about one or two houses."

"*Housing projects* I should say. And even more may be going up," Felix said slowly. "That you-know-what is planning to build *two* housing projects here in El Norte. He says he doesn't like the idea personally, but he wants me to know that nobody can stop the wave of the future."

"He's wrong," Laura said, surprised at her own vehemence. "But I assume that he won't try to go through with it if you can prove that El Norte can and should be saved."

"That's what he hinted," Felix acknowledged.

"Don't you see the point, then, dear? You have to come up with the best report that any man has ever seen. You've got to give them plans and a positive program to save El Norte, and you'd better do it quickly."

"Y-yes...yes, you're right, of course." Felix looked down at the scrambled sheets on the desk in front of him. "Yes, of course."

But he sat down slowly and looked around in vain for his ball-point pen.

"It's on top of the *Atlas*, silly," Laura said patiently. Then she added, "That man Clymer jokes about so many things, he might very well be joking about this, too."

"He definitely wasn't joking," Felix said. "He told me that both land parcels had been owned outright by Gordon Ulric, and that he now plans to go into partnership with Gordon with the idea of destroying our agenda. I can understand why Clymer is doing this. After all, he himself says that he's got no real attachment to the place and is just looking to make a few quick bucks. But I can't understand Gordon taking a part in the destruction of everything. Why, Gordon has lived in El Norte all his life."

Laura said slowly, "I suspect he's bitter about your not having married his daughter."

"Oh, right!" Anger flamed brightly again in Felix's eyes. "He'll damn well have to get used to it—and to hell with him!"

At least Felix seemed to be past his self-imposed paralysis,

Laura saw thankfully. These stormy moments had emphasized how exhausted she was from having to plan everything for the wedding by herself in such a short time.

She turned to go, and saw Selina standing quietly in the library door. Felix's mother had been watching the two of them and taking in all that they said. Now she gripped the crook of her cane more tightly and gestured down the hall.

"You," she said to Laura. "The other room."

Laura walked back into the salon. She had intended to stand during her confrontation with Felix's mother, but she was so tired she sat down on one of the soft chairs instead. She closed her eyes and waited. The tap-tap of Selina's cane came closer down the hallway. The door of the room was suddenly shut, and the tapping sounded as if it was beside the chair. Laura opened her eyes. Selina was seated so that the two women could face each other across the cocktail table.

"You handled that incident with Felix very well indeed," she said, paying Laura her first compliment grudgingly. "He gets these tantrums occasionally—as you must know by now—and someone has to hear him out and settle him down."

"I understand that."

"He was always a good, quiet boy," Selina went on. "But every so often he'd become so angry that he was beyond words. A woman can go to her room and cry, but Felix doesn't have that type of relief available to him."

Laura wondered if Selina allowed such relief for herself. In a crisis, this woman would probably try to shout down the opposition and demand that matters be handled the way she wanted them. She was the sort of woman who would charge into all opposition; and it was puzzling to Laura that Selina should be talking almost pleasantly to someone she'd probably have liked to poison.

"I want to make my position clear beyond all dispute," Selina said. "I don't approve of this marriage on such short notice and to someone Felix hardly knows. On the other hand, I have to admit that I find Gordon's recent behavior so abysmal, that if Felix suddenly wanted to marry that girl of his, I think I'd scream the house down."

Laura said, "I take it then that you aren't going to oppose our marriage."

"No, but when you two begin having your first big arguments, and I'm sure you will, I promise you I'll tell Felix that he's getting what he deserves because he married against his mother's wishes." Selina held up one hand to stop Laura from protesting. "One of the privileges of being old is that you can second-guess your children for not having done what you advised them to do."

"Why are you telling *me* this?" Laura's voice was icy. "I intend to do my best to see that what you predict doesn't happen, whether you make threats about it or not."

"What in the world has Felix done to deserve so much loyalty from any human creature?" Selina asked suddenly."

Laura said after a pause, "I don't want to be rude, but I've been terribly busy today and there are any number of other things that need to be done before I can go to bed."

"Sit back," Selina said with so much authority in her voice, that Laura obeyed in spite of herself. "We can talk about the preparations in a little while. It occurs to me that you'll have no friends or family at the wedding and that you will be, and actually are, all alone in this world."

"I'm perfectly all right."

"That's hard to believe. It's unfortunate that no one close to you can take you into a corner and tell you about the good and bad parts of marriage and what follows. You really are an innocent child, with no mother to guide her."

"Would you want me to be guided and warned, Selina, or pushed around?"

"Pushed around, my dear, and told in no uncertain terms exactly what to do," Selina admitted. "Youth is indeed wasted on the young."

"Really, you must excuse me," Laura began.

"No, I will not excuse you! Sit down here and listen to me. I want to talk to you about—well, about calamities."

"I don't understand."

"You will if you listen." Selina shuffled her cane from one hand to another. "Everybody is calamity-prone, Laura, and you shouldn't expect eternal happiness. A wife or a husband is a hostage to fortune and as a result you become more vulnerable, no matter how hard you try to fight it."

Laura understood that Selina must have battled vigorously against the inroads of capricious fortune in her life. The battle showed, in her lined face, her gray hair, and even in the cane, which she must have adopted with bitterness and loathing.

"I realize," Laura said slowly, "that you've started to believe that I'm in love with Felix and you're trying to warn me that our future won't be perfect. I ought to thank you, but I don't want to think about future calamities. I'm sure you can understand that."

"All my men have been calamity-prone," Selina went on as if there had been no interruption. "I've been widowed twice, you know, and in a sense, Harvey has been taken away from me. He's perfectly polite. He's well-behaved. He even has a good deal of skill at tinkering with gadgets. But he practically admitted last night at the dinner table that he has left the world, so to speak, as my husbands have done, but in a different way and even more effectively."

Selina cocked her head to one side to help bring her thoughts together. Those sharp eyes never left Laura, silently commanding her to stay where she was.

Laura could understand that for Selina, the only true, close relative left to her was Felix, and that she dreaded losing any part of her control over him.

"You say that all your men have been calamity-prone," Laura reminded her swiftly. "Do you think that for Felix to marry me would be a calamity as well?"

"Felix is prone to trouble in other ways. He's been reasonably normal up to now, but he very nearly destroyed his future several months ago during an argument that I'm sure could have been avoided somehow. You might be able to take care of him very nicely up to a point, but Felix may be lost to both of us if he goes beyond that point."

Laura said firmly, "Felix isn't nearly as difficult as you make him out to be."

"Then I think we understand each other in spite of your blind loyalty to my son," Selina remarked. "I've been trying to tell you, in a roundabout way, that Felix is unusually difficult and that his happiness may hang by a thread. Any personal remarks I've made about myself will be forgotten by each of us." And from her manner, it was plain that she really expected Laura to forget everything she had said that wasn't about Felix.

"There is only one other thing for us to talk about," she added. "I'm not going to let Gordon and Janice know that I didn't approve of this marriage and cause all the gossipy tongues to waggle by not making an appearance. Now, tell me what preparations you've made for the wedding."

Laura paid no further heed to unpleasantness of any description. She took a deep breath and launched into a full-scale review of her plans and accomplishments.

Selina listened as if carved in stone. No sign of consent or disapproval passed her lips. Laura thought she was probably trying to keep from showing her resentment that so much had been done without her having had control over it.

"I shall, of course, give my son away," she said when Laura was finished. "I'll march with him to a point ten feet short of the altar. Is that clear?"

Laura nodded. It wasn't quite the way she had planned it, but she knew better than to try and overrule this strong-willed woman. The important point, though, was that Mrs. Page would take a part in her son's wedding, thereby tacitly giving her blessing (in public, at least) to the match.

Laura couldn't help feeling that matters were going to work out very well. Very well, indeed!

CHAPTER SIX

The ceremony wasn't scheduled until two o'clock, Sunday afternoon, but things already had started to go downhill by eleven that morning.

Laura had been commanded upstairs by Selina, in a voice that would brook no disagreement whatever. Several local women, called in by Selina early, went up with her to help her to fit the dress on, and they burbled happily all the while. For her own peace of mind, Laura talked to Felix on the house phone during a pause in the fitting, just to make sure he wasn't getting upset or irritated. As she couldn't possibly know what was happening downstairs, she was spared the sight of sheer chaos.

For one thing, the extra folding chairs that were supposed to be sent over by one of the neighbors simply didn't show up. Harvey, because his fear of cars was so acute, could not be dispatched to retrieve them. So Felix was forced to make the trip himself, along with one of the yard men. As it happened, a number of the chairs were so bent out of shape they were useless, so Felix went to yet another neighbor's house in hopes of picking up enough additional chairs to fill the void.

The caterer had arrived that morning on time, but the quality of the food wasn't up to Selina's liking, and she quickly gave the man a piece of her mind, adding that he was to do "whatever it took" to see that the difficulty was corrected. All this took valuable time away from the other necessary preparations, and by then, Laura's nerves were stretched taut.

A local clergyman, pressed upon by Selina at the final

moment, arrived and spent some time conferring with the bride-groom-to-be. Felix had pulled every string possible in order to cut the usual waiting time required in Florida between taking out a marriage license and the actual ceremony. Still, there were the usual last-minute formalities that needed his attention. After his session with Felix, the Reverend Mr. Watson went upstairs to speak privately with Laura.

Laura's mind was on almost anything else, than the questions he asked her. She gave so many muddled responses, in fact, that the clergyman's questions took much longer than would have been the case otherwise. By the time Laura, dressed in the gown she had purchased at the last minute (which thankfully fit her petite frame beautifully), was ready to make her way downstairs, it was already half-past one, and only thirty minutes remained to her.

To add to her unease, Susan took this moment to mention that some of Felix's boyhood friends had "cornered him" downstairs and were teasing him about all his former sweethearts and his new "ball-and-chain." The maid insisted he seemed to be taking the kidding in good humor, and Laura could only hope it was true.

The day had started out with threatening weather and, indeed, just as the onrush of guests was reaching its climax, rain started to pelt down. A bolt of lightning whitened the sky and the parched ground.

"The perfect touch," Laura told herself ruefully, as she waited impatiently in her room upstairs for her "curtain call." "It's nature's version of one of Felix's blasts of temper. I hope Felix isn't as jumpy about all this as I am."

The guests, including those who had been at the meeting earlier in the week, poured into Coralton, along with the rain. But the conversation that ensued wasn't nearly as jovial as the gay chatter that most of them were accustomed to making while taking part in local weddings.

The women were gathered together in pairs or small groups, apparently so they could speak without being overheard.

"Oh, it's a beautiful house, all right, but I've never been too fond of these vintage places."

"The house is expensive, of course, but this wedding can't be costing Selina too much money. It's a rush job if ever I saw one."

"Selina seems resigned by all this to me.... Did you notice?"

And the men made one remark after another about "another good man going down the drain" followed by other offhand comments:

"Might as well be here in this weather because I'm sure not going to get any fishing done."

"I was hoping to try out some new golf clubs today, but there's no chance of it now."

"While you guys are stopped by the weather, I can always go where it's warm and sunny—my greenhouse. Do you know, there's one flower really hard to grow once you've planted it, and that's the rhododendron? It's a fact. My wife got me interested in horticulture, you know."

"You're too old and creaky to play golf these days, Charlie, and you know it as well as I do. Seriously, though, is it true what I hear about you planning a merger with—?"

Finally, to everyone's relief, the pianist struck up an anticipatory medley and the room came to an expectant hush.

Laura had been in an anteroom behind the parlor with Ned and his wife, Barbara. The painter had been looking through the furnishings of the house, especially the paintings.

"Not a single 'Boyer' in the place," he muttered. "Talk about bad taste."

"Selina prefers classical pieces," Laura said, peeking into the larger room as it was slowly filling with guests.

"Vermeers!" Ned Boyer exploded. "A Vermeer is a bad investment because you can't be sure whether it's an original or if it was painted by that Dutchman who forged so many Vermeers during the Second World War."

Barbara sighed wearily. "Oh come on, Ned. Can't you forget about business for once in your life."

"You're the matron of honor today, not me. I still have to get my hands dirty up to here when we get home."

Barbara smiled wearily. "Let's have one of our real old-fashioned knock-down and drag-out arguments, so we can show Laura what married life is really li— Oh, Look who just came in. The practical joker himself."

Laura leaned forward to see Oscar Clymer, his head held rigidly straight and blinking furiously as though his contact lenses were giving him a difficult time, raucously greeting everyone he knew in the room. He paused before a seat next to the center aisle.

"Felix hates him," Laura said. "It's a shame he was included in the general invitation."

Harvey entered the anteroom, tapping at his right hand pocket and smiling even more widely than usual.

Laura stopped him before he could wander back into the ballroom. "Do you see that fellow over there, Harvey? The one who's holding his head so straight?"

"Yes, sure. Do you want me to call him over for you?"

"No. What I'd like you to do is make sure he doesn't sit on the aisle. Please, Harvey. I don't want Felix to see him when he walks to the altar."

"Okay," Harvey nodded agreeably. "I'll just ask him to sit further away and tell him why. I'm sure he won't mind."

Laura blinked in horror, but before she could grab Harvey, he had walked past her and into the ballroom.

In desperation, Laura turned to Ned who had been watching the interplay in amusement. He nodded and went after Harvey. He caught up just in time to hear Selina instructing her first-born son:

"You're going to be the best man, so you have to stay with Felix. Go find him right this instant."

"Mother, I just have to take a minute to—"

There was only one way of talking to Harvey, it seemed, if results were wanted quickly. Selina stamped a foot and commanded: "Now, Harvey. Now!"

It was a close call, but Harvey turned around and hurried out of the ballroom. He shrugged helplessly at Laura when he passed her and then hurried up the stairs to join Felix.

Laura heaved a sigh of relief and turned once more to the problem of Oscar Clymer's too-close-to-the-aisle position. She peeked once more through the crack in the door and saw with relief that Ned was on his way over to Clymer with a resolute look on his face. The two of them shook hands and chatted for a short time, and as soon as she realized that each man was on his feet Laura felt sure that Ned Boyer had enough finesse not to let matters get out of hand.

The piano player suddenly unleashed a number of loud chords, one of them jibing with a flash of lightning outside. Rain slanted down and thudded against the windows on the northeast side of the house.

"Upstairs with you," Barbara said cheerfully, pointing to the back stairs. "I'll let you know when it's time to make your appearance."

Laura glanced through the partly-open door and saw Ned easing his way toward the aisle seat before which Oscar Clymer was standing.

"I just want to make sure—" Laura started to say.

"There's no time for that," Barbara said. "Ned will take care of that jerk. Now hurry!— Thank heavens, we're moving at last!"

"Your husband's a dear," Laura said, hurrying back upstairs to wait for her cue.

"Believe me, he's acting solely out of enlightened self-interest, I'm sure," Barbara said, grinning. "He'll probably do his darnedest to get some stock tips from the guy—or sell him some paintings!"

Following the attention-getting intro, the pianist deftly segued into "Here Comes the Bride." Laura could hear the men's foot-steps descending the stairs. To control her excitement, Laura turned and gazed out the window at the green-tinged beauty of El Norte, proudly taking the rain to itself and seeming to gird its forces against the majestic thunder and lightning.

Then Barbara opened the door. "Now!" she whispered, as she lightly stepped out into the hallway and blew a kiss with her fingertips.

"Good luck, dear," she whispered. "Good luck from all your family and friends who couldn't be here."

Laura eased the veil over her face and lifted the bridal bouquet. Only a few more minutes now, she told herself. The ceremony wouldn't take too long, she supposed, and then Felix would raise her veil and kiss her. The two of them would walk back down the aisle and into the reception room. People would welcome them cheerfully to married life, and others would come over to Felix in that slightly embarrassed manner to hand him envelopes with their checks inside. Felix would tuck the envelopes into his breast pocket and heartily shake hands with the giver.

It would be just like a dozen and one other weddings she had seen, after all: only this one was hers and Felix's.

And yet she couldn't seem to concentrate on the magnitude of it. She was in the hall now—and then on the stairs. The smell of fresh varnish pierced the sweet scent of the flowers she held lightly in her hands. She suddenly noticed that the carpeting seemed to have been slightly loosened on one of the steps, and her shoe wavered; another quarter-inch, she thought in panic, and she would have tumbled down those stairs. Perhaps even this old house was opposed to her marriage!

As she reached the lower steps safely, she again was startled to hear loud words being exchanged in the ballroom. Harvey, from his position at the front of the room, was leaning over and talking directly to Oscar, who was sitting next to the aisle after all. It was Felix who finally pulled Harvey away and back over to where the clergyman waited.

Laura could only imagine what Harvey had been saying, and shuddered. Oscar Clymer hadn't budged. He looked red-faced but self-assured in spite of his obvious embarrassment. Behind him, also next to the aisle, Ned waited patiently to forestall any more trouble. Laura learned afterwards that Ned had success-fully edged Oscar out of one aisle seat, but that Clymer had simply moved up and taken the aisle seat in the row before him.

Laura was distracted by another savage crack of thunder. She exchanged glances with Barbara and followed her with measured paces into the room she wouldn't leave until she had become Mrs. Felix Page.

Selina, contrary to the rehearsal plan, had taken her place at the exact spot where Barbara, as matron of honor, had been instructed to stand. Barbara slid smoothly into place beside her, but Selina's position, right next to Laura, gave the impression that she was giving both the groom and the bride away. It was not a usual arrangement, and one that was sure to set the women to gossiping furiously when they conducted their portmortems the next day.

Felix, Laura supposed, must have been in the seventh circle of hell, not only because of his shyness in a crowd, but also because of the *outré* behavior of his mother and brother. Still, he managed to smile comfortingly at Laura as she joined him in front of the makeshift altar, flanked by tall baskets of sweet-smelling pink and white flowers. The clergyman moved forward and began to speak in dulcet tones about the sanctity of marriage, its difficulties and joys. *This can't be my wedding,* Laura thought in a sudden panic. *It's happening so simply and quickly.*

At the appropriate moment, Harvey proudly reached into his vest pocket and removed the ring, a family heirloom, consisting of one brilliant star sapphire set in platinum and surrounded by a wreath of diamonds. It had been gleaned, with her bless-ings, from Selina's jewel box, and Laura thought she had never seen anything quite so beautiful. Felix didn't immediately reach out for the ring, so Harvey moved forward, as if he himself had been designated to put it on Laura's hand! Felix stopped him gently, taking the time to touch Harvey reassuringly, then placed the ring carefully on the third finger of Laura's left hand.

The few words which would bind them together for life were

exchanged; Felix spoke in measured husky tones and Laura in the clear, well-modulated voice which had brought her such favorable notice on the stage. Felix lifted her veil and hesitated. He stared into her blue eyes, shining brilliantly like the sapphire. They seemed frozen in time, like the miniature couple nestling in the creamy frosting at the top of the ornate wedding cake waiting in the next room.

The clergyman whispered, "Kiss her, for heaven's sake, man! She's your wife now!"

Felix kissed her tenderly. The audience applauded happily, as if no one had ever been kissed at the altar before—as if it were an ingenious idea.

The pianist struck up the triumphant "Wedding March." Felix gave Laura his arm as they started to walk down the aisle. Laura leaned towards him, whispering as they walked.

"Do you feel different, now that we're married?" she asked.

"No, not a bit. You?"

"No. It's funny, but I don't feel a bit different." Abruptly she added, "I hope there isn't going to be any trouble with Harvey."

"I warned him not to look at Clymer during the recessional, and to keep out of the man's way."

"That's a relief. Talking about near misses, Felix, I nearly tripped on the rug coming down the stairs. If I'd been walking a little bit faster, I'd have fallen smack on my face."

Felix looked concerned. "Really? I'll have to have the handyman take a look at it. Funny, I don't recall it being loose before. Well, I'm certainly glad you *didn't* take a tumble. That would've made this 'interesting' wedding even more memorable, don't you think? Besides I would have had to deny having any acquaintance with such a clumsy girl—God Almighty!" He looked down into her happy face with joy. "I love my clumsy girl!"

It happened swiftly, and no one in the wedding party could have guessed what Oscar was going to do when Harvey, squiring Barbara just behind the happy couple, passed Clymer in the aisle. But what Oscar actually did was to strike out at his recent tormentor with another childish practical joke.

Harvey, following strict orders from Felix, as well as from his mother, hadn't said another word to Clymer when he approached the other man, although he had glanced sideways, as he told Felix afterwards, and moved slightly closer to the middle of the aisle so that he wouldn't be in close proximity to the man. But Clymer, still fuming from the earlier incident, simply thrust out a foot and tripped Harvey. Harvey called out with surprise and fright and then went sprawling. The top of his head cannoned into Laura's back, and he struck the floor as she and Felix whirled around to help him. Barbara jumped to one side and saved herself.

It was Ned who intervened when Felix, furious at Clymer, stretched out both hands and tried to close them around Clymer's neck. Clymer called out and fell backwards. A glassy tinkle rang out against an uncarpeted stretch of floor as one of his contact lenses struck it. A series of warning shouts rose from the other guests.

Laura rushed to Felix. As she grabbed his right shoulder he flicked it back in order to dislodge her. It was Laura's first test of her new husband's brute strength, and it was one that she was unlikely to forget. For the first time, as she reeled back, it occurred to her that she hoped Felix would never become as angry at her as he was at this moment at Oscar Clymer.

This man of hers—she hated to think it, but it seemed to be true—could pose a life-and-death danger to someone he hated.

PART TWO

CHAPTER SEVEN

"I'd swear that there's moonlight shining all around us," Laura said, puzzled, "but there's no moon out tonight."

"What did you say?" Felix was lounging in a yard chair opposite her. He was preoccupied and looked across at her in surprise.

"I was just wondering how there can be moonlight out here, but no sign of a moon."

"Because, my dear girl, I hired a landscape architect to get that effect," Felix said. "And because I just now pushed a few buttons before we came outside. The lights are so tiny you can hardly see them. They're mostly hidden out there on the trees or behind the bushes."

"You do get the effect of moonlight and its subtle shadows, though," Laura said appreciatively. "It's very restful."

Felix sighed. "I wish I was so restful."

"What's wrong, dear?"

"I'm still worrying about preventing the building schemes in El Norte. There couldn't be anything else wrong, Laura, believe me."

She smiled at him fondly. "You told me you had worked out a plan that's sure to keep El Norte safe from the developers."

"That's right, Laura, I have."

"Well then, if you've worked out the plan, why on earth should you be upset any longer about it?"

"Because—well, can't you guess?"

He straightened up, and she looked quizzically at the sharp

features which had become so familiar to her over the last few weeks. Laura had spent several days in New York, closing up her apartment and arranging to have the rest of her belongings shipped to Coralton. Before the wedding, she had phoned her director to explain why she wouldn't be returning to the company. He had wished her well, but she could sense reluctance in his voice as he said "Just take care of yourself, kiddo. And keep in touch. You'll always have a place here, ya' know."

"Thanks, Bill," she had said sincerely. "I'll do that." But she was thankful there was no need to spend any further time with the theatre people during this short trip. Felix had used the days since their wedding prowling El Norte while he refined his plans to keep the area intact.

During these few days, Selina had insisted that Laura and Felix move into the adjacent wing of Coralton. Except for the fact that they were all serviced by the same kitchen staff, it was like being a next-door neighbor. Selina avoided talking to Laura any more than was necessary to issue orders only thinly disguised as suggestions.

Harvey had been relatively quiet, too, in the last few days. The only subject on his mind seemed to be the humiliation he felt he had endured at Felix's wedding.

"How could that man have done such a thing to me?" Harvey asked during one dinner, his eyes wide with shock.

"Why not put it out of your mind?" Felix said wearily. "His throat probably still hurts him and his shins had been kicked black and blue before he left the ballroom."

Selina snapped, "Change the subject, Harvey, by all means. You're beginning to sound like a broken record."

Harvey obligingly tried to talk about something else, but his words were halting and his train of thought seemed disjointed, and he soon left them to retreat once more to his cellar hideout.

Wedding presents were still coming in from out-of-town friends and relatives. One of Laura's former foster parents sent a broiler, which she certainly didn't need at Coralton, but the idea of their thoughtfulness moved her to tears. She sat down and wrote a long, heartfelt thank-you letter, forcing herself not to remember the unkind incidents she had endured while in that particular couple's care.

She was beginning to understand, too, why newly married people say that they can no longer recall what it was like to be single. When she woke up in the morning, Felix was at her side. They shared their breakfast as companions, and at dinner they told each other what had happened during the day. They both had come to realize that nobody else in the world meant as much to either of them.

They had even endured their first mild disagreement. One night, while they were in bed, but not yet asleep, Laura began talking in detail about a furniture change she was planning. Felix had suddenly yawned and turned his back on her to prepare for sleep.

"Are you tired already?" Laura had asked in exasperation.

"I've had a full day." Felix half turned back toward her. "Why is it, do you suppose, that women talk so much in bed? Or why do you suppose they save the things that are most important to them to discuss late at night when all a man wants is some sleep?"

Laura couldn't help asking how he'd found out so much about women's bedtime habits. Something in the tone of her voice alerted Felix to the error in judgment he'd made, and he quickly pointed out that his previous experiences all had been acquired before he knew her. Laura took her time, but grudgingly forgave him at last. And she was so artful about it that Felix didn't realize that he'd been kept awake until after two o'clock. As soon as Laura pointed out her small triumph, though, he grinned good-naturedly, turned away from her once more, and promptly fell asleep. Laura tossed and turned for another half hour before sleep overtook her.

But on this Wednesday evening, for the first time since their wedding, fear for her new husband and for herself soared again to the surface of her mind. And from that time onward, the fear wouldn't be dispelled.

"You're right, of course, Laura," he said. "I think I have figured out the only possible way to keep El Norte pristine. I suppose it was floating around in my head all this time, really, but it only became part of my consciousness a few days ago."

"Then there shouldn't be anything to worry about." A wisp of Laura's blonde hair straggled over her forehead and she pushed it back in place. The steel of the yard chair gleamed in the artificial moonlight.

"What's bothering me now is the presentation," he said. "I'm so keyed up over this that, at the first sign of dissension, I'm liable to make a beeline for somebody's throat."

"Felix, you can't go through your whole life allowing yourself to lose your temper at the slightest provocation."

"I haven't always been like this, Laura, no matter what you may think. It's just that saving El Norte is more important to me than almost anything else you could name."

"Then it seems to me you have to make a point of not losing your temper, no matter what happens."

"I can't seem to control it. If one of those idiots asks a single question or makes one hostile remark, I can predict I'm going to haul off and let the damn fool have it where it hurts."

"Then why don't you arrange for a 'plant' in the audience, as we say in show biz? Go to Ned Boyer, for instance, and give your presentation to him first. Then when you talk to the whole committee on Friday night, Ned will already be on your side. You'll have an ally in the audience."

"Ned's a successful painter, of course, and well-to-do because of it. But people around here think he's a little out of his league trying to be a business entrepreneur as well. I just don't know how much they'll be willing to follow his lead on this." Felix rose from the yard chair and began to pace nervously back and forth across the swath of lawn. "The most respected man of the bunch is Gordon, who's not only a banker, but it's just my luck he's now become heavily involved in this housing scheme of Oscar's."

"Well, this plan of yours has got to be good enough to sway

him, too."

Laura said it more out of loyalty to her husband, than certainty, so she was shocked when Felix suddenly whirled around and stared at her as if he'd never seen her before.

"Laura, that's absolutely genius! I'm sure Gordon loves El Norte every bit as much as the rest of us do. He can't still be so mad at me for not marrying his daughter that he'd want to risk destroying all this. He just can't be!"

Without further discussion, Felix turned and ran into the house, closing the door firmly behind him. Laura, who was so short she could sit swinging her feet in the 'moonlight,' without touching the ground, allowed herself to enjoy a rare moment of contentment. She finally had what she had always wanted: marriage to a good man with roots in the land and a respected family name. She had found all of it at last, and she could only hope that it would go on forever.

The main house door opened and shut again. Felix walked back out to her slowly.

"Did you call Gordon? What happened, dear?" She sensed that she ought to feel uncomfortable, without exactly knowing why.

"Oh yes, I called him," Felix said in a strained voice.

"Felix, what happened?"

"When he heard my voice, he sounded cold, like ice. I told him what I wanted to talk to him about, and he said that nothing I could tell him was going to make the slightest difference as far as he was concerned."

"But I *know* you're right," Laura said. "He *has* to hear you out."

"Oh he'll hear me out all right...."

"But you said that there's nothing he'd like less."

"He doesn't know it yet, but he's going to hear me out whether he likes it or not."

Her discomfort changed to a flick of fear. "What do you mean?"

"Gordon's giving a dinner for some of his banking buddies

tonight, he told me. He mentioned it as an excuse for not wanting to see me. But I'm going over to his place and nag him until he gives me ten minutes alone."

"No, you mustn't do that!" Laura had stood up now and was facing him. "Gordon will never listen if you try to force him like that."

He smiled. "No, you misunderstand. I've barged into Gordon's house a million and one times over the years. I know the place backwards and forwards. Once I'm there, he'll listen to me all right."

Laura said decisively, "Then I'm going with you."

"No thanks, Laura." Felix was adamant. "Let me handle this on my own please."

"Felix! I can't let you do this alone!"

He turned his back to her and walked to the garage. "I'm not going to lose my temper," he said.

"I know you wouldn't do so on purpose," Laura said. "But Felix, I'm begging you to take somebody along. If not me, then at least take someone."

"Who would you suggest, Laura? Mother is in bed by now. Harvey won't ride in a car; not since that infamous accident of his. That leaves the maids, the cook, the handyman and the gardener. Who should I take?"

"Felix, all I know is that you shouldn't go out there by yourself." Laura reached up a hand toward him. "Why don't you call Ned? Perhaps he could go with you. All I know is that if I were Gordon and I wanted to make trouble for you, I would annoy you in the presence of witnesses, and when you made a lunge at me, I'd have you arrested for assault. That's what I'd do if I were Gordon, Felix. On my word of honor, that's what I'd do!"

"I doubt it. Gordon would never want to appear in court, let alone admit publicly that he couldn't handle me." Felix bit his lower lip in frustration. "But I'll promise you this; no matter what happens, I won't lay a hand on Gordon. I give you my solemn oath, Laura. Now, you can relax and go to bed. I haven't got the slightest idea what time I'll be back." And with that, he turned and walked away.

Laura watched his figure grow smaller. In less than five minutes, the sky-blue Rambler roared out of the Coralton garage. She watched it until there was nothing left to see but a curl of exhaust smoke then walked into the house.

In the main wing's family room, as she might have expected, Harvey sat watching an old black-and-white movie on television. He was sprawled carelessly across a comfortable sofa and cradled a big bowl of popcorn next to his chest.

"Have some popcorn, Laura? It's very good—it has melted butter on it." He licked a finger thoughtfully. "This is an old movie, but if you want to watch something newer, I'll put that on, instead."

Laura said she didn't care what she watched. Harvey began telling her the names of all the actors as the shadowy images flickered about on the screen. He pointed to a program listing lying crumpled near his chair.

"This is a *really old* picture and most of the actors in it are dead," he informed her. "It was made the same year my mother married Mr. Page, and we changed our names."

"Harvey," she said unable to maintain her silence any longer. "Felix has gone over to Gordon Ulric's place...."

"I'll bet he took the Rambler." A wince of pain flashed across Harvey's usually bland pudding of a face. "I won't be comfortable again until he gets back without an accident—knock on wood. I can see why you're so worried."

"I'm worried because Felix might get angry enough to hurt Gordon."

"Felix wouldn't do that, Laura. Honest, Felix doesn't go around hitting everybody who doesn't agree with him."

"But this isn't a little disagreement that he's having with Gordon," Laura said. "Look, Harvey, I know you'd hate to do it; but can't you go out there with me for your brother's sake? Just this once? I'll be glad to drive you over and wait in the car."

Harvey didn't answer. He seemed galvanized by what was happening on the screen. "Look, look! Clark Gable's car is going to go over that cliff, Laura!"

He suddenly leaned forward and switched the set to another channel. He was breathing with considerable difficulty, and a moment passed before he was able to look back at Laura.

"If you'd rather watch the Clark Gable picture, Laura, I'll turn back to that."

"No, that's all right." She sighed, and looked at his shaking hands. "Forget it, Harvey. Forget everything I just said."

Laura waited until midnight. Then she stood up and returned to the bedroom she shared with Felix. It was a big room, and with the double bed pushed over to the wall, there was plenty of space for her to walk up and down without banging her shins on anything. Even better, the noise wouldn't disturb Selina who had probably taken a sleeping pill, as she generally did at eleven o'clock, and gone to bed.

At a quarter to one, Laura heard stealthy steps on the stairs. She climbed into bed, picked up the book on her night stand, and pretended she had been reading.

Felix opened the door quietly. When he saw that Laura's light was still on, he closed the door and sat down on his side of the bed to remove his shoes.

"Felix, what happened?" Laura couldn't hide her concern. "Did anything happen?"

"For all practical purposes," he muttered, "I might just as well have stayed home as you wanted me to do."

He was pulling off a shoe as he spoke, and she noticed a fresh abrasion across the knuckles of one hand.

"How did that happen?"

"Don't worry." He stood up and reached for a bathrobe. "You have so many of your clothes jammed into the closet that I may have to put all my things in paper bags and keep them under the bed."

"Felix, *please!*"

He smiled at her. "Well, at least Gordon isn't going to complain about anything in court."

"You *did* hurt him? In spite of what you promised me, Felix, you hurt him? I can hardly believe—"

The smile disappeared. "I'll tell you *exactly* what happened, Laura. I went over there and cornered him. I told him he was going to have to hear me out eventually, so it might as well be sooner, rather than later. Then he could come up with any answer he thought plausible, before I tell the whole story in public. Believe me, Laura, at that point I was being as reasonable as hell."

"'*At that point*'," she repeated tonelessly. "Go on...."

"Well, at his suggestion, we went into his library, and I gave him my pitch. He listened with an icy smile on his face the whole time. You would have thought I had come in for a loan without any collateral. You'd never have guessed that I was merely asking for his help in saving the area where both of us have lived most of our lives."

"It's all right, Felix. You can do it in spite of him," Laura said firmly. Still her eyes returned to the nasty cut on the back of his right hand. "But you still haven't explained that cut. Did you do anything to Gordon tonight, Felix? Please be honest with me."

"Don't be silly, Laura." He walked into the adjoining bathroom where his voice echoed harshly against the tile as he admitted to her what had happened.

"I realized immediately that Gordon is out to make as much trouble as he can for me, and he couldn't care less if he destroys El Norte or not. He might hesitate for a while if he were on his own, but with that jerk, Clymer, fronting for him, there's no limit to what mischief he's liable to come up with. *Damn* him to hell and back, Laura!—"

"Felix, please don't keep me in suspense," she pleaded. "Just tell me— *How did you get that cut?*"

"Well, as you can probably realize, I got angrier and angrier at him. He was being so vindictive about everything that I couldn't even talk properly. My throat actually choked up. I made fists, trying desperately to control myself, but I swear I was ready to pound him into the wall. Then I remembered the promise I made to you. I knew then I couldn't—and wouldn't lay a hand on him. I got up and started walking around and around the library, trying to work off the fury inside me."

She felt a wave of relief wash over her. "So you didn't hit Gordon after all?"

"No, I never touched him," Felix said. "What actually happened is that I spotted a favorite vase of his, one of those pricey little Ming things, perched like a bird on one of the side tables—and I just picked it up and smashed it against the floor. A small chunk of it flew up and cut me on the back of the hand, Laura, that's all that happened. Of course I offered to pay for it—and had to write out one whale of a check before I left, but it was worth it, in a way, to have used that vase as a surrogate for my anger. Much better than hitting Gordon, wouldn't you say?"

"I'd say it *was* worth it, if it kept you from losing control. Never mind the cost, dear," she said, settling more firmly into her side of the bed. "It could have been a lot worse."

"I'm not so sure. What could possibly be worse than a completely wasted trip?" Felix went back to the key problem. "I'm right back where I was before I went over there."

But the next day, Laura and Felix discovered that his talk with Gordon hadn't been a waste of time—though not how either of them expected.

CHAPTER EIGHT

Laura was sitting at a table in what was called "the summer room," writing thank-you notes for the gifts they had received. She took a fresh piece of stationery out of the newly-delivered box and brushed a forefinger lightly along the printed line near the top: *Laura Page*.

Halfway through the sixth note, she heard the door opening behind her. Laura looked up and turned her head. Selina, dressed in a pale gray dress that matched her hair, stomped into the room, slamming the door behind her.

Laura started to smile and make some trivial remark, but one look at the older woman's forbidding face stopped her. Selina went to a large window and stared out, her grayish figure blocking most of the Coralton yard from Laura's sight. She lifted her gaze to the rugged wilderness of the El Norte region beyond, with its wild greenery and one of the quaint wooden bridges in the foreground. From here, the side of the landscape seemed as remote and formidable as a deserted island.

Laura shrugged and attempted to return to her note-writing, but the tip of Selina's cane thumped petulantly against the checkered floor tile, interrupting her train of thought.

"You must never again give Susan permission to use her own judgment about the clothing she will wear when we loan her out to one of the neighbors," the older woman said abruptly. "It's so important that a servant look well and, in my experience, maids have no sense about that sort of thing at all."

As Selina spoke, Laura's right hand jumped involuntarily,

and a squiggly line of black ink appeared on the paper. It didn't bother her that she'd have to write the letter all over again, but she felt a genuine pang of regret at having to throw out even one sheet of the precious new stationery with her married name on it.

"Susan, as you know, was asked to help out with the Ryerson children this morning—*as Felix wanted her to*—as a return favor for the folding chairs they loaned us for the wedding," she pointed out. "From what I've seen of her, she dresses sensibly and tastefully, so I merely told her to use her own judgment about what to wear while she's caring for the children. Felix assured me that the affair was expected to be very informal. I doubt if she'll have much contact at all with the adults."

"Don't make the same error again," Selina said sharply, ignoring Laura's reasonable explanation. She sat down with great care, putting the cane across her thighs as if it was a naughty child about to be spanked.

"I may decide," Laura said, more casually than she felt, "to ask Susan to wear a sarong when she waits on Felix and me. I'm sure he would enjoy it."

"It's *not* a laughing matter!" Selina shouted.

Laura caught herself short of saying that nothing at Coralton seemed to be a laughing matter. Everyone in the house overreacted, whether it was Harvey refusing to ride in a car, or Felix going for somebody's throat if he didn't get his own way. Now here was Selina laying down the law as if their futures depended on it.

"It is ludicrous, I agree," Laura said evenly, "but it's definitely not a laughing matter."

Selina chose to ignore this comment. "As long as you do things correctly, we'll get along," she said, and turned to leave the room.

The phone rang before Laura could say anything in response, and she hurried into the next room. The extension had been placed on a library shelf that jutted out at what would have been eye level for most people but was just above that point for her.

Laura lifted the receiver, reached over to pull a French provincial chair away from a Spanish table, and sat down to answer:

"Hello?"

There was a split-second pause, and then a man's voice, but high-pitched and disguised to sound like a child, asked:

"May I speak to Mr. Page?"

"Which Mr. Page?"

"Mr. Felix...."

"Who's calling, please?"

"*I* am." The self-assurance in his voice gave away the man's identity; Laura immediately knew that she was talking to Oscar Clymer, and she supposed that he was disguising his voice by way of another one of his foolish jokes.

"Felix isn't here right now, Mr. Clymer," Laura said evenly. "I'll have him call you as soon as he gets back."

"Mr. *what*?" Clymer's voice slipped back to its natural level for a moment, but swiftly lurched up again: "*You* don't know who I am and I never heard of you neither, so there. I'll call him again later...."

The connection abruptly was broken at the other end and Laura sighed in vexation. She returned to the summer room to finish her letters and was making real headway, when Felix came in for lunch. He had been trying to line up his ideas in some kind of logical order for the presentation he was scheduled to make the next evening. Almost everybody he would speak before was a long-time friend, but Felix was nervous and wanted to get his thoughts organized as carefully as he could.

"A busy morning?" he asked cheerfully, taking note of the pile of completed letters. "Just as soon as I'm through dealing with this El Norte business, Laura, I'm taking you to Hawaii for that delayed honeymoon."

"I'm looking forward to it, dear," she said happily.

"Anything else going on?"

"You had a phone call from Oscar Clymer."

"From—?" Felix scowled. "What in the world does *he* want?"

"He refused to tell me. In fact, he kept insisting he *wasn't*

Oscar Clymer! But I knew better—I recognized his voice."

"He can take a flying leap—" Felix said dismissively. "What's for lunch?"

"You can't just forget it like that," Laura said quickly. "Maybe Clymer wants to discuss something positive for a change. You ought to give him the benefit of the doubt."

"He probably wants to demonstrate a new joke or something, and he's *so* enthusiastic he doesn't care who he shows it to." Felix shook his head fiercely. "He's just like a little kid, for heaven's sake. You wouldn't take a one-year-old seriously, would you?"

"Foolish or not, he *is* in partnership with Gordon to ruin El Norte," Laura reminded him. "He may have something important to tell you about all that."

"To hell with him then! I refuse to have anything to do with that miserable creep."

Laura rose and took him by the hand. "Come along, dear."

He didn't realize what Laura intended until she stopped in front of the telephone in the next room. Then he drew back sharply.

"Now don't try to push me around like this, Laura. Believe me, I've taken enough pushing around in my life, and I won't put up with any of it from you."

"Darling, you know as well as I do that it's only common good manners to talk with the man. You'll have to do it sooner or later. Why not get it over with, now? At least find out what he wants."

Felix frowned, but didn't leave the room, so Laura picked up the phone and made contact with the Clymer home. Oscar was on the line in a few minutes.

"County morgue," he boomed cheerfully. "The customer is always dead. Ha-ha!"

Felix let out a deep sigh and with a look of disgust, took the receiver out of Laura's hand. She stood close enough to listen. She held his free hand closely in her own.

"This is Felix Page. I understand you phoned me a little while ago."

"Yes, I did. Your wife is a great little recognizer of voices, I must say. I've fooled plenty of other people with that imitation of mine, but I couldn't get away with it with her."

"I wonder if you'd tell me...," Felix started carefully.

"Of course! You want to know why I called. I admit I kept hoping your brother would take the phone and I could bug him just a little—in fun, of course! Your *half*-brother, you know—actually, though, it's about this other business."

"I don't understand a word you're saying!"

"Well, *Gordon* tells me you did some high, wide, and fancy talking to him last night."

Laura felt Felix suddenly squeeze her fingers tightly.

"So—what about it? What has that got to do with you?"

"To tell you the truth and nothing but, I want to know exactly what you said to him. I've asked and asked Gordon, but he practically foams at the mouth whenever your name comes up."

"What are you saying, Oscar? Are you ready to double-cross your partner?"

"Gordon is working out a grudge, you know, young man, and the whole thing is almost entirely your own fault as far as I can tell." Clymer chuckled mildly. "But what I want is to find out exactly what you're proposing to tell everyone at Friday night's meeting—so I can come up with an appropriate rebuttal. That's a perfectly fair statement to make, isn't it?"

"You ought to be able to get it from Gordon, if that's all you really want."

"The point is that if your ideas are as Gordon has hinted at, well, I wouldn't say that I might not be interested in that line of reasoning, too. After all, I did come to El Norte to live, and I don't want to see the countryside messed up any more than you do—if you can figure out some sensible way to stop the developers. If they can't be stopped, though, I'll be in line for the first pick and shovel. Otherwise, who knows?"

Felix picked his words carefully, "This isn't one of your so-called practical jokes, is it?"

"No, Mr. Page. Not this time."

"Because if it is...," Felix started.

"Oh-oh, here comes the violence again."

"You can probably understand why I'm suspicious."

"Uh-huh, but not why you're so intent on hitting people. In my case, I'll admit I gave your brother a hard time at the wedding, though as far as I'm concerned, he damn well had it coming. I think you gave me a hard time back—with interest. I can still feel those hands of yours on my windpipe."

"I thought you'd hurt Harvey pretty badly," Felix said calmly. "I was just protecting him—and I didn't realize it was only his pride that had taken a slamming."

"Well, he hurt my pride, too, by asking me to sit away from the aisle so I couldn't be seen—and saying it so loudly that everybody heard it. I was minding my own business up until that point—but one bad turn deserves another, don't you know?"

"I'll agree that we may have gotten off on the wrong foot." Felix said reasonably. "Look. I would be happy to come over to your place right now and explain my plan for saving El Norte in detail."

"Oh no, you won't!"

"Whyever not? You're at home, aren't you?"

"For a while."

Well then, what's wrong? Are you afraid Gordon has got some spies watching you?"

"Uh-uh," Clymer said. "What I'm afraid of is those hands of yours."

Felix turned red with embarrassment. "Listen here, Oscar, I don't blame you for feeling that way. But believe me I promise not to get out of line. I'll just talk to you, explain my overall plan, and leave. That'll be it. You don't even have to tell me what you think of it."

"No deal, Page. You aren't going to talk to me here at my place. That's a guarantee."

"We can go over it right now on the phone or I can call you again at whatever time suits you."

"I can't go along with that either, Page. To tell you the truth, I like to see somebody's face when I'm talking to him, especially about something as important as this. People have been known to lie, you know; I've done a bit of lying, myself. But when I'm looking somebody in the face, by God, I can tell if I'm getting the straight story."

"Then we'll have to meet somewhere in public."

"Looks like it," Clymer agreed. "I'll tell you what. Do you know a restaurant called Amalfi's?"

"That Italian place in town? Yes, I know it, but I don't think they open until five."

"Then I'll meet you there at seven-thirty. Will you come?"

Felix sighed. "Seven-thirty it is, Clymer. Goodb—"

"No! Wait a minute!"

"What now?"

"It just occurred to me, Page, that whether it's in public or not, you still might act up if we're sitting there alone."

"I'm telling you that's not going to happen. I won't lay a hand on you. Take my word for it, will you?"

"Let me just finish, Page. I was going to say that, from having talked to her recently and having seen her in a few difficult situations, your wife seems to me like a pretty level-headed person. She ought to be able to control you if no one else can. Bring her along...."

Felix hung up without another word. He pulled his hand away from Laura's.

"It's a good thing I'll have a handler with me tonight. I guess I can't be trusted on my own."

"Darling, I didn't invite myself," Laura pointed out reasonably.

"This whole idea is ridiculous!" Felix snorted. "Am I going to have to take you with me every time I go out to talk with somebody about a building? Maybe you should bring a dog collar and leash with you tonight."

"If you tell me to stay home and not go with you, I'll do it."

"You know I can't afford to have you stay home. What will I do if Clymer takes one look at me sitting there alone and walks out?"

A third voice interrupted them:

"You're going to see that awful man—Clymer?"

Laura whirled around to see who had been eavesdropping on their conversation. It was Harvey, of course, who often prowled from room to room in search of distraction. The blandly amiable look that was generally plastered across his thick features had been replaced with a calculating frown. "You know what that man did to me," Harvey continued. "He made me look like a fool in front of all your friends! How can you have anything to do with him after that?"

Felix smiled at his brother gently. Laura had noticed that he never said a sharp word to Harvey or showed him any of the embarrassment or distress that generally led to violence on Felix's part.

"You know that I've been trying to keep people from building in El Norte and turning it into another Miami Beach," Felix explained patiently. "I need Clymer's help with that, and I can't get it if I refuse to talk to him."

"I should think you'd try to get help from somebody else— somebody nicer," Harvey said stubbornly.

"I would, if there *were* anybody else. Clymer is Gordon's partner, but he might switch sides if he's handled just right."

Harvey put a hand to the back of his head and shook it as if he was trying to forget a bad dream. "I think I'll go down to the cellar and do a little tinkering, I guess," he said, as if Felix hadn't spoken. "At least if a machine does something bad, you know it isn't trying to hurt you *personally.*"

Felix walked Harvey to the door and stood holding it open with his hand outstretched. Laura understood that what he was doing was part of a ritual with roots in their childhood.

"Friends, Harvey?"

There was a pause. Harvey Page looked from side to side as if he wanted to dodge the issue, but finally he straightened and held out his own hand toward his half-brother.

"Always friends," he said robotically as his part of the childhood ritual.

But he left the room without another word or even a look back at his half-brother, or at Laura—and he was still frowning.

* * * * * * *

The El Norte area lay in the inner portion of an irregular letter G, Laura began to realize, as they sped along Florida 3. She looked out at the hard and rugged beauty of this paradise in which she now lived and which was becoming such an integral part of her.

The county seat of Apocalypse was located approximately half an hour from the Coralton estate. Main Street was a typical resort area, a hodgepodge of bingo parlors, hot dog stands, burlesque shows, and movie houses. A guess-your-weight concessionaire called invitingly to them from in front of a row of theatres as Felix turned off the main street and into a smaller one. Felix closed his eyes tightly but briefly after he had parked the Rambler.

"What you just saw," he said, "is the opposition."

"Excuse me?"

"This is the sort of tourist trap that most of El Norte could turn into if we stand by and let it happen."

"Not all resorts are as vulgar as this one."

"And I've seen a lot that are worse," Felix said irritably. "Let's go meet Clymer so we can get out of this hellhole as soon as possible!"

Amalfi's, located next to the Apocalypse Hotel, was a popular watering place. Felix escorted Laura under a wide green awning and into a cool, dimly-lit place with tables covered with snowy white linen and greenery-edged candles in hurricane lamps as centerpieces. An aging female pianist with big blowsy hair was attempting to entertain a sparse crowd by playing and singing obscure songs from various Broadway musicals. She was a teensy-bit off-key.

The *maître d'* gestured them with a flourish to a table at the center of the room. No more than a dozen people were here, most of them gathered around the gleaming bar. Laura heard the soft tinkle of a drink being shaken thoroughly and a few raucous laughs, and suddenly realized that she found these city-associated noises depressing, after even such a short time in the quiet paradise that was Coralton.

The pianist finished her set and waited for the applause and tips that didn't come. She gazed round the room a moment, sighed stoically, and launched into another half-hearted selection.

At half-past eight, Felix called over the waiter, a tall man dressed inexplicably in a bright green shirt, white jacket, and blue pants.

"Do you know a gentleman by the name of Oscar Clymer?"

"The 'joke man'? Sure I do," the waiter answered. "Whenever he comes in, he leaves a pretty good tip. Of course I remember him."

"Well, my wife and I were supposed to meet him here a while ago, and I wonder if he might be playing one of his jokes on us?"

"I never heard o' him doing that, but I'll ask Lou if he knows anything about it."

The waiter headed to the bar and came back a short time later with an envelope. Inside it was a letter handwritten on hotel stationery.

"Page: I'm sorry I can't keep our appointment tonight, but one of my company's new toys is part of a lawsuit for copyright infringement and I'm having a meeting with my lawyers before a court appearance tomorrow. Give me a buzz at home tomorrow morning. I definitely want to see you before the evening meeting at Ned's place. My best to your little lady—literally in this case, ha-ha!—Clymer."

Laura had been reading the note over Felix's right shoulder. She sighed, touched Felix comfortingly and said to him:

"I suppose we'd better just go."

"One more round, Laura," he said. "I don't want word to get around that Clymer gets to decide whether we go or stay."

"Apparently he couldn't help what happened."

"I don't believe a word in that note."

"You mean you won't even give Clymer a chance to come over to our side?"

"Oscar Clymer has played a joke on me for the last time." Their drinks arrived, but Felix paused as he started to raise the glass to his lips. "I don't think I want this after all—we've got that long drive back."

There was an anemic potted plant drooping against the wall near them. Felix stood up, drink in hand, and wandered over as if to examine it. When he came back to the table, his glass was empty.

"We can't let that waiter think I can't hold my liquor, can we?" he said with a grin. "As soon as you're finished with your drink, Laura, we'll be on our way—and try to forget we got suckered into this trip."

CHAPTER NINE

Laura tried twice more to persuade Felix that he ought to get in touch with Oscar Clymer on Friday morning, but Felix refused. After lunch, he went into the library to begin the final draft of his presentation. He had been there for only a few minutes when the phone rang.

Laura picked it up on the extension and heard Clymer on the other end, already deep in conversation with Felix. She half-smiled to herself and put the phone down gently, so she wouldn't interrupt them.

She was discussing a possible change in the electrical wiring with Harvey in the summer room when Felix entered. He frowned at his brother, sprawled ungracefully across one of the easy chairs and Harvey stood up promptly with an awkward smile.

"I can see that you want to be alone with Laura," he said. "I'll go down to the cellar."

He left the room before Felix could politely—but untruthfully—say he needn't go.

Once Harvey's steps had faded down the hallway, Felix said quietly: "Clymer talked me into another get-together, just before this evening's meeting. This time," he added, "he wants us to pick him up at his place about half past six."

"That's fine with me. What did you tell him?"

"I said he'd better be on the level this time," Felix said shortly.

In the waning rays of the sun, Oscar Clymer's sprawling concrete house looked as if it had been constructed from soft, gray wool. He was waiting on the front patio as Laura and Felix pulled up in the Rambler, and waved at them cheerfully. He wore a white suit, a rakish straw hat, and green-tinted sunglasses, which, Laura supposed, were meant to protect his contact lenses. He finished sipping a clinking glass of ice water as he waited for them.

"Ned's house isn't too far from here, over that little bridge and across the sand canyon." He gestured vaguely. "I don't mind stretching my legs after sitting in court all day," he continued. "What say we walk over?"

"I think I'd rather drive...."

"Uh-huh, but if you get upset at me you might try to run us off the road. No, thanks, Page, we'll walk—if you want to have that little discussion we talked about...."

Felix sighed heavily, but didn't argue. He carefully parked under Oscar's carport. Laura got out and was dismayed to discover that, once she stepped off the pavement, her high heels immediately sank part way into the sandy soil, putting a terrific strain on her ankles. She hoped Felix wouldn't notice her discomfort and be distracted, so she let him walk ahead of her as they joined Oscar along the pathway heading out across the expanse of scrub.

Oscar began talking about his major interest: his beloved practical jokes.

"I test each and every one of 'em, personally," he said. "People are always sending new ones to me, sometimes anonymously, and any that look promising, I spend a couple of weeks carrying it around and trying it out in different situations. My business requires a certain amount of dedication to the theme, don'tcha know."

Felix led them down the path: "Let's get a move on—I don't want to be late for the meeting" he said.

They walked roughly side by side, Oscar was a foot or so ahead and Laura, struggling in spite of the problem with her heels, was slightly behind Felix.

She was listening so carefully to the conversation between

the two men, that she hardly paid any attention to the dazzling scenery around her. The huge orange ball that was the setting sun kissed oases of lush greenery and expanses of bare, rugged earth alike. Sand that clustered in rough circular patches, like huge sightless eyes, overlooked the quirky wooden bridges which spanned the sandy canyons and serviced the network of walking trails through the region. But Laura's concentration darted from Felix to Oscar and back again as they spoke.

"Even Laura hasn't yet heard my basic plan of what's needed to save El Norte," Felix began, "but I'm prepared to give it to you now, point by point. Number one: there will be no widening of the highway. That's important, I think, because it would destroy this view," he gestured expansively about them, "and then in a short time we'd have popcorn sellers in the canyons under the bridges."

"Uh-huh," Oscar nodded. "I agree with you. But you have to give way on something, my friend, because the pressure against you is too strong. What are you willing to give up for El Norte?"

"That brings me to my next point," Felix said. "Number two: some expansion of El Norte State Park should be allowed. After all, everyone in the country should have the right to come out here and enjoy all this, too. It might be possible to develop another one of the beaches for concessions; maybe even a marina for boats."

"Now. What about new construction? I'm a landowner out here and suppose I *want* to develop it."

"Number three: no new housing construction shall be allowed within the boundaries of the El Norte district. It means standardizing the zoning laws, for a start, but I think it can be done. And it ought to put a finish once and for all to Gordon's ideas of putting in a new project."

"Gordon's real motive, I believe, was to bug *you*, and I really doubt if he expects to be allowed to put up any kind of a big project." Clymer rubbed his chin thoughtfully. "Me, I've got a slightly different notion. What if Gordon and I began constructing a number of two-story single-use residences?"

"No!" Felix said promptly.

"Now wait.... You aren't thinking straight about this," Oscar said. He had taken what looked to be a plain rubber ball, about the size of an orange, out of his pocket and was squeezing it as he spoke. Instead of resisting the pressure of his hands, however, the "ball" crackled like paper and thinned out, flat as a pancake. Oscar rolled it back to its original shape between both hands, chuckling as he did. "This is one of the little projects I was telling you about that I just received anonymously in the mail. I think I could package this like a standard baseball. It may not be a bad little number for my line, I think," he added, partially to himself.

"We *were* talking about development in El Norte," Felix said impatiently.

"Yes...yes, of course, I'm sorry...." Oscar reluctantly tucked the rubber ball back into his jacket pocket. "It is possible, I think, to build a number of smaller houses close together in El Norte," he went on, "and not disturb any of our precious views."

"And after that, you will put in shopping facilities to accommodate the people living in those houses," Felix said sarcastically "A shopping center, parking lots—and all that goes with it. People will demand the convenience and, if they buy into the area, they are entitled to a voice in it, after all. It's only reasonable. Meanwhile, El Norte goes to hell in a handbasket...."

"You could prevent some of that from happening, though, if you could standardize those zoning laws," Oscar pointed out.

"And any newcomers are going to put on pressure to have *those* zoning laws changed back again," Felix snapped.

"I don't know. I think the oldtimers would probably win, if it came to a fight over the zoning laws." Clymer grinned. "What's more, the new people may not want El Norte mucked up, either, once they got in and saw what we have to offer."

"I still say there's no place for a planned community in El Norte." Felix said brusquely.

"For heaven's sake, man!" Clymer gestured with a hand raised upward. "Any rentals would be skyhigh. You'd get the same upper-income types that you have now, only their homes would be smaller, and they'd own less of the adjoining property— *And* they'd be concentrated in a relatively small proportion of the area."

Felix said, "I know that's been done in other areas of the country, but there's got to be at least one region that's left pristine."

"Maybe we can cut ourselves a deal," Oscar said, as they reached one of the quaint wooden bridges. "Here's what we can do: you stick in that part about putting up some smaller houses and I'll go along with the rest of what you want."

"I won't sell myself down the river...," Felix began.

"Stop and think it through now," Clymer said persuasively. "I'm on the *other* side of the fence, and if I agree to your point of view and change sides, it's going to be quite convincing to a lot of people at that meeting tonight. Correct?"

"Yes, but only if you're willing to agree with my entire plan and forget about new construction of small houses."

"You have to pay a price to make converts," Oscar said. "Why, I'd even go along with you on the subject of keeping these nasty little bridges intact, if that's what you want to do— though personally, I think they're pretty damned dangerous...."

Later on, when it was a matter of vital importance to recall exactly what had transpired during the brief walk, Laura could close her eyes and "see" everything that had been going on at that particular moment.

She had been plodding along carefully beside Felix. Several feet away, and closer to the flimsy railing of the old bridge, Oscar strode with a cheery confidence in his every step. His shoes kicked up some of the sand scattered across the wooden planks.

"This is a pretty damned dangerous thing we're walking on right now," he said again and, as if to emphasize his statement, he brought his hand down hard against the wooden rail.

At that precise moment, Laura heard the unmistakable "*pop-pop-pop*" of three rapidly-fired gunshots. Felix, acting so quickly that she wasn't able to see much of what happened next, reached around with one hand to pull her toward him and protect her body with his own. But she was able to get a glimpse, past Felix to the side, where Oscar Clymer, wavering, lost his balance and fell heavily against the railing.

There was a *cr-rack* of wood giving way, just as Felix reached out with his free hand to grab Oscar. She sensed, rather than heard, Felix's hand snatch uselessly against Oscar's jacket. Clymer shouted out unintelligibly. His voice gradually faded, until suddenly, it seemed to Laura, it stopped with the sound of something heavy striking the canyon sand below.

Total silence followed. Felix held a shivering Laura tightly, and she was grateful for the warmth and comfort that his nearness provided.

His voice seemed to float gently downwards as she fought to maintain consciousness. "We're going to walk now to the end of the bridge. There are two thick utility poles there, Laura, and you're going to stand between them while I go down into the canyon to see if I can do anything for Oscar. Ready?"

Steeling herself, Laura made herself obey his command. But it wasn't until she stood alone between the two thick, scarred old wooden poles did she begin to worry that her husband might be putting himself in danger from the unseen sniper.

Felix moved with grace and speed, allowing the sand to hurtle him downwards to the canyon bottom. Oscar Clymer lay on his back, facing skyward. The tinted green glasses he'd been wearing had disappeared during the ghastly fall.

Felix hesitated briefly before touching Oscar, then gripped the prone man's hands just above the wrists, and set a palm down flat against the victim's heart. He raised Oscar's eyelids, then slowly stood and turned away. Though Laura was crouched at the top of the canyon some distance away, she could still sense the immense sadness in her husband.

It seemed impossible for Felix to climb up out of that canyon without help, but she realized he'd probably been doing it since childhood and knew the tricks involved. He was with her in less than five minutes, his face a stony mask.

"You don't have to tell me what shape Oscar is in." Laura said, "I can guess."

"We were just talking," Felix remarked wonderingly. "Just a few minutes ago we were having a decent conversation, and now he's dead."

"Was he shot? I mean, did you see any wounds left by the bullets?"

"No," he said. "I didn't see bullet holes nor was there any blood on him. But he must have been shot...." Felix was beginning to regain his poise, and he was breathing almost normally. "We'll go over to Ned's house—it's closer—and phone the police from there."

"All right. Whatever you think best...." Absently, Laura brushed at Felix's dirt-encrusted jacket.

Felix shrugged then smiled at her as he helped brush the dirt off his pants. "It's funny when you think of it," he said. "A man gets killed and seconds later here we stand, brushing my clothes off, as if that mattered at all...."

"And you spend time philosophizing while somebody brushes your clothes," she said.

"Death makes philosophers out of foolish people who manage to stay alive," he said, and suddenly whirled around to face her. "Let's rest a few more minutes, Laura, before we go," he said, searching her pale face anxiously. "Ned's place isn't more than twenty minutes from here...."

But it was a quarter to eight and nearly dark before they finally reached the Boyer place. Laura, who had struggled silently through the sand with her heels half-immersed, sank down gratefully on the piano bench in the long entry hall as Felix rushed to find the phone.

Laura vaguely heard Barbara questioning her why she seemed so upset. Upraised voices in the next room sounded like surf pounding on a distant shore to her muddled brain.

"What's Felix doing?" one person was asking.

"And where's Oscar?" Gordon suddenly put in. "He isn't here

yet, either—or maybe he's just hiding in the closet to surprise us." A brief burst of laughter was the response.

Laura shuddered. Barbara stood nearby and waited to hear what Felix was going to say on the phone. Finally, everyone in the house seemed to sense the urgency of the call he was making.

"Emergency? This is Felix Page in El Norte. I must report a death. I'm at the Boyer home, and if you pick me up here I'll take you to the spot.... Yes, I know who the victim is. His name is Oscar Clymer.... Someone murdered him. I'll give you all the details when you get here.... Yes, of course I'll wait for you."

Barbara winced. She was wearing a trendy black and red chiffon outfit, and even her clothing seemed to shudder in apprehension.

"Not again," she whispered. "Please, God, not again, Felix!"

Laura, still weak and dizzy from the impact of what she had witnessed, was able to say sharply:

"Felix had nothing to do with this, Barbara!"

Barbara's voice became more conversational. "Of course not, sweetie—*if you say so.*"

She turned to peer into the alcove where Felix had gone to place his call, and that motion gave Laura more than enough room to see into the living room that faced it. Perhaps a dozen people, all of whom she had seen at various times since the last weekend, were seated there, talking in low voices amongst themselves and glancing awkwardly at each other as well as toward the door. Several seemed embarrassed at the sight of her, and a fresh wave of whispering arose.

Felix dropped the receiver into its cradle and took half a dozen steps toward the living room. He stopped suddenly and turned to Laura in the entry hall: "Are you all right, honey?"

"F-fine."

"Are you sure? No shivers and shakes?"

"Nothing I can't control as long as I need to...."

Felix's eyes darted towards Barbara. "Would you get some whiskey for Laura, please? She's had a terrible shock."

Laura couldn't help but notice that Barbara subconsciously drew back when Felix moved towards her, as if she wanted to avoid all contact with him.

Felix shrugged and turned back toward the living room. The random whispering stopped. Silence ruled. Except for Felix's footsteps, there might have been no one else inside the room.

Barbara gave Laura a pitying look and said, "I'll get that drink for you. Just a minute...."

She moved down the hall to the kitchen.

Laura stood up and moved slowly toward her husband's side. Her ankles began to ache as soon as her feet touched the floor.

"Well," Felix said to the stony-faced group. "What's been going on? Ned, are you in charge here?"

Ned blinked. His lips opened, but after a pause they snapped shut.

"What in hell *are* you people up to?" Felix asked even more loudly. "We can save El Norte, you know, and I've got the detailed plans to prove it—right here in my pocket. That's what this meeting is about, isn't it? I was delegated to come up with a plan and I've got one. What more do you people want from me?"

A white-haired man with an unlined face, a former United States Senator, cleared his throat, but said nothing. An auto executive, who commuted to Detroit by private plane and had earned millions for his company in a number of cut-throat deals, looked down at both hands folded tightly in his lap.

Laura, leaning sideways against the wall, said to her husband, "They think you did it, Felix."

"Did what? You mean that I shot Clymer? But the shots came from a distance. And I was right next to Clymer when the shots were fired. You all know me—Do you people really believe that I would shoot a man in cold blood?"

No response—from any of them.

Felix drew a batch of typewritten sheets out of his jacket pocket and dropped them on the checker-patterned floor.

As he turned to leave Laura looked past him and called out

in as clear a voice as she could muster: "You're a pack of fools, the whole lot of you!"

Felix gestured to her to be quiet, pulling her tiny hands into his larger ones. She succumbed to the rough warmth before realizing how tightly he held her. With only a little more pressure he could have hurt her.

"Let's wait outside for the police."

"Yes, of course."

As they started outside, Barbara rushed toward Laura with her whiskey on a tray. Seeing Felix at Laura's side, though, Barbara stopped short. Laura looked longingly at the drink, but refused it and walked proudly, head held high, with her husband through the door.

CHAPTER TEN

"Let me tell the two of you, one more time, exactly where you stand," said police lieutenant Vogel, swiveling around to face them.

The hours that had passed seemed as long as several years in confinement. Not that Laura had been confined at all. She had ridden with Felix and two uniformed policemen back to the scene of the crime, and waited with them while help was called. An ambulance from the morgue had arrived finally, clearly outlined against the dim horizon. She had then been driven in the police car to the town of Apocalypse to the gray concrete building that did double duty as police headquarters and court house.

Laura had been questioned alone for a time. But not until she found herself in this wide and well-lit office, was she permitted to rejoin her husband. Felix seemed calm, but a telltale pulse was visible in his right temple.

Lt. Charles Vogel lurked behind a paper-cluttered desk He was a tall man, in his late forties, with a sprinkling of gray hair at the sides of his bullet-shaped head. He seemed to have no lower lip, judging from a casual glance, and was probably the only man in El Norte whose face remained untouched by the sun.

His questions had certainly been polite at the start, and his voice was soft in spite of its insistence.

"Now that you two have been questioned separately, I wonder if we can get together and connect what we know?" he began.

"Mr. Page, you had been wanting an interview with Oscar Clymer for some time?"

"No, it was actually the other way around." Felix was forcing himself to be patient. If the two of them had been close enough, Laura would have touched him in reassurance.

"You mean that even though he had you by the short hairs, so to speak, he wanted to see *you?* Why, Mr. Page?"

"To propose a deal. He was willing to persuade Gordon Ulric to put up smaller houses instead of big estates, provided his plans met no opposition from me or anybody else who wants to keep El Norte pretty much the way it is."

"Had Clymer discussed any of this with Ulric?"

"Not as far as I know. But I can't be positive."

"Ulric denies any knowledge of it." Vogel's bright blue eyes probed Felix skillfully. "How does it happen, Mr. Page, that you and Mr. Ulric are such enemies? The man had absolutely nothing good to say about you over the phone."

Laura tried to forestall Felix's rage from becoming apparent to Vogel: "What connection does *that* have to do with Mr. Clymer's death?" she interrupted.

"We'll get to that in time," Vogel said briskly, dismissing her query with a wave of one calloused hand.

"Mr. Vogel, we've answered all your relevant questions and have done it without a lawyer being present. We have nothing to hide about the murder, and I would think it's obvious that we didn't hurt Oscar Clymer in any way. I don't feel that my husband or I should cooperate any further without getting legal advice."

"Do you refuse to answer questions about your relationships with Gordon Ulric?" Vogel persisted.

Laura snapped, "Do you refuse to tell us why it should be so important?" She could sense Felix's growing frustration.

"I'm an official who's doing his job," Vogel pointed out. "I don't have to answer you people in any way at all."

"Not unless you want our cooperation," Laura pointed out.

"I suppose," Vogel said, looking from husband to wife; "that the two of you figure this whole business is pretty straightforward. Isn't that right?"

Felix, weighing his words carefully, said, "I don't see why you'd have any problems clearing my wife and myself from any suspicion. Clymer was shot, and your people can tell whether or not the bullets came from a distance."

"That's true, we could. But there'd be nothing to prevent you from having shot Clymer from a distance and then saying that you were with him at the time he was shot. I'm sure your wife would back up your story."

"No." Felix sat up straight, his eyes flaming with intellectual inspiration. "But there's another factor, you know. Laura and I were walking with Clymer on the bridge, and all of us made—"

Vogel suddenly smacked his hands down across the desk. "This has got to stop! We're sitting here playing games, exactly as if you two hadn't told the craziest single lie I have heard in my entire career!"

The pulse beating in Felix's right temple flared sharply. His hands clenched quickly, and then slowly opened.

Laura said flatly, "You'll have to explain that statement, Lieutenant."

"The only thing I *have* to do is make sure I'm doing my job," Vogel snapped. "I'd hate to arrange it, frankly, but detaining the two of you wouldn't pose as many problems as you seem to think it would."

Felix rumbled heavily, "*Am* I 'detained,' Lieutenant? Or under arrest?"

Vogel picked his words with care. "I'm the one asking the questions, if you remember."

"You sound as if I'm *not* under arrest, Lieutenant. In that case, my wife and I are going to leave your delightful company and go home."

Vogel said quietly, "Stay where you are, my friend, or you really will be in a jam worse than anything you've ever known in your life."

Felix rasped, "Let's see what happens if you try and go

through with that."

He pushed his chair back, obviously expecting to get up from it.

Laura called out, "Felix, don't do this!"

He stopped and edged back slowly, his hands rising in the air until they were at shoulder level. He paused then slammed both fists down against his kneecaps. He didn't wince from whatever pain he may have felt from the blow.

Laura said to the lieutenant, "I think we're entitled to know what you mean by calling us liars."

Vogel hesitated, glancing down at his cluttered desk and absently straightening some of the papers. A picture-frame had fallen over on its face, and he righted it, revealing a photograph of a pretty young woman and three sturdy children. Only by listening to his slow and even breathing was it possible to realize how tired he had become.

"Your story is that you were walking on one of the wooden bridges when you heard three shots fired very quickly. Then Clymer lost his balance and fell through the railing and into the canyon below. Is that right?"

"Of course," Laura said. "You know all that. It's what we've both told you numerous times."

Vogel's eyes flickered as he moved his bullet head in Felix's direction. "Well now, Page, did you find any bullet holes on Clymer's body when you climbed down into the canyon to examine him?"

"No. And I didn't *examine* him—not like that."

"Neither has our medical examiner," Vogel said. "The reason is that *Oscar Clymer wasn't shot*."

As Laura looked at Felix in wonder, she saw that he was staring back at her, not in anger, though, but in fear.

Laura turned back insistently to Vogel. "But we *heard* the shots and we saw him lose his balance and fall right afterwards."

"I've had some men scouring the area for bullet casings, but so far they haven't found a thing." Vogel was brusque. "The story you two are telling doesn't add up."

Felix stood quickly, turned, and started to the door, then glanced around while waiting for Laura. His face was pale, she saw, and his jaw was jutted with fierce and silent anger.

As she got to her feet in one graceful motion, Vogel said with surprising mildness, "I only have one more point to make, and then you both can go."

But even as he was speaking, Laura hurried to Felix's side. When she looked back at the lieutenant, her right hand had already found the comforting warmth of her husband's left.

Vogel noticed it, of course. "Two points, actually, I should have said. No arrest is going to be made in the Clymer killing at least until the autopsy has been finished. It should be done by tomorrow."

Laura said quickly, "I don't see what the autopsy can possibly prove. My husband and I were walking on the wooden bridge with Mr. Clymer and we all made footprints while we were on it. Those prints have to show that Mr. Clymer lost his balance and fell. And you yourself say that Mr. Clymer wasn't shot...."

"If that's your idea of conclusive proof...." Vogel started then shook his head several times with eyes shut tightly. "After six hours without sleep you get so that you're not able to see too straight, let alone to think right. I'll put it to you this way, though: When the autopsy results come along, I'll get 'em to you personally—to both of you. In the meantime, I'll talk the situation over with my bosses."

Felix opened the door halfway and stepped back to let Laura go through in front of him.

"My second point," Vogel called out, the words stopping Laura in her tracks, "is that, in my opinion, Mrs. Page might be in a desperate situation."

"I?" Laura gripped her husband's hand tightly. "What do you mean? That doesn't make any sense to me, Lieutenant Vogel."

"What I mean, that your husband is a man with a temper. A hothead. A man whose actions in the past have brought about at least one man's death and who has carried on pretty savagely from time to time when he doesn't get what he wants. My point is that you, of all people, should—"

Laura refused to listen to any more. She marched through the door. But Vogel's voice, raised only slightly, carried well.

"I'm warning you, be careful, Mrs. Page," he said. "Your husband may get angry at you sometime, and then, I predict, you'll have to fight for your life. If there's anything you should want to tell me at any time—and the sooner the better—you can always reach me at this offi—"

Laura and Felix were across the large old-fashioned ante-room by the time Vogel's crisp voice no longer seemed to be tracking them. Felix's footsteps rang in her ears as he led the way outside. As she followed his sturdy back, Laura told herself that she had never loved her husband as much as she did at this moment.

It was late Saturday morning by the time they reached home in the car that Felix, with police permission, had retrieved from Oscar Clymer's property. Laura promptly went up to their bedroom to try to get what she hoped would be a few hours sleep at the very least. As she was closing the windows against the late morning sun, she heard Felix talking urgently to someone, probably his mother. She couldn't make out any of his words.

But Selina's tones were clear and firm as she said, "The first thing you should have done was to get in touch with our lawyer."

Felix said something else to her, but Laura couldn't quite hear.

"You're *not* automatically guilty because you get in touch with a lawyer," Selina told him with her usual firmness. "Next time—if there should be a next time—don't hesitate to call the lawyer first and let him take charge."

Felix joined Laura in the bedroom a few minutes later, muttering that he'd probably never be able to fall asleep. But not long after he turned away from her in bed, he was sleeping like a baby. Laura, on the other hand, lying flat on her back for several hours, couldn't sleep at all.

A bath and a light snack did very little to revive her. She was smearing a pat of butter across a piece of toast when she reminded herself that the autopsy was being performed (or had it been finished by now?) on what was left of poor Oscar—and promptly lost her appetite.

Felix stopped wolfing down a couple of soft-boiled eggs long enough to ask her if anything was wrong.

"I'm all right," Laura said with more ease than she felt. "Don't worry about me."

Felix retired to the library after their light meal and tried to make plans for the future of what he had ambitiously labeled "The El Norte Project." Selina was issuing orders to the cook for that evening's dinner and Harvey joined Laura in the living room where he chattered away about his latest experiments.

"I took the phone apart to see how it all works," he was saying eagerly. "It's really an elaborate device. Now let me explain what my invention is supposed to do. Say that I'm out of reach of a telephone and you need something from me and you want to get in touch. So what do you do? You dial a special number on your telephone, and a minute later, this thing I carry starts to buzz like crazy. That's when I go to a phone and call you—and then you tell me what you want. Isn't that simple?"

His heavy features glowed while he extolled the simplicity of his idea. There wasn't anything else on his mind, obviously, except to entertain Laura for a few moments; and she doubted if he remembered or even cared that Oscar Clymer lay dead by violence.

"Excuse me," she interrupted him wearily. "There's something I need to see about." Harvey, with his usual politeness, stood up as she left the room.

Laura made her way back upstairs to bathe her temples and try to get a little rest before what she had been told would be a dinner party including two "very special" guests.

* * * * * * *

"I understand you've been having a difficult time of it lately, Felix," Jack Noland said. "Actually, in my view, there's only one thing you can do about it."

"Give up?" Felix said with a smile.

"Of course not!"

They were seated around the grand old refectory table in the dining room, Selina at one end, and Harvey facing her. Laura and Felix had been placed together at one side of the table; Jack and his wife, Evelyn were at the other.

Noland was a successful oil company executive who lived part of the time in El Norte—when he wasn't traveling in the Mideast to various oil-rich countries. His stories about the high living of certain sheiks, in contrast to the near starvation of the native populace, were told well and entertainingly, but with an underlying seriousness that made his own feelings clear. He was sensitive enough not to try to be too funny about such matters, and he had steadfastly refused to involve himself in the El Norte controversies. He had invited himself and his wife to dinner at Coralton on this particular evening after they returned for another few weeks residency. He was a tall, dark-haired man in his mid-thirties, with the squinty eyes and leathery skin of someone who spent a great deal of time in the sun.

Evelyn generally went with him on his trips, although her Jewish background could make for a few problems with the locals, since she insisted on being truthful on all the forms that she was asked to fill out. As a result, she would occasionally find herself being treated as a suspected spy for the State of Israel. She was a tall, bright-eyed woman, with hair the same color as burnished copper. She obviously enjoyed her husband's company, listening to him as avidly as if she'd never before heard the particular story he was telling. It was easy to see that Evelyn and her husband were not only man and wife, but good friends and companions as well. Laura found herself drawn to the couple, and looked forward to expanding their friendship.

Felix, in the natural pause between the appetizer and soup courses, spoke up earnestly, "If there's anything you can think of that I can do to push this El Norte project forward, Jack, I wish you'd tell me what it is."

"Fight," Jack replied.

"Not *literally*, I hope," Selina put in. She was dressed in a pale blue which lent her aging skin a delicate rosy cast. "He's tried that, and you can believe me when I say that it doesn't work."

"Listen to me," Jack said. "The State Highway Commission wants to widen Florida Three. *Fight them.* Go down to their hearings in Jacksonville and lay it on the line once and for all."

"Do you mean you think that I should go down there on my own?" Felix said, slightly apprehensive, yet thoughtful. "The people here won't support anything I say or do, as long as Clymer's murder hangs over my head."

"They're not organized enough to object to you going, though. The so-called 'Group to Save El Norte' has disintegrated. There isn't anybody left who can come up with a feasible idea. Someone has got to step up if any plan is to be carried out."

"There'd be a lot of publicity." Felix frowned down at the table. "What'll I do if one of the highway commissioners asks me something like, 'Aren't you the man who killed two people in arguments about El Norte's future?' I'd sure as the devil say something wrong again, Jack."

Selina rapped the table decisively with a closed fist. "Just tell the truth and shame the devil, Felix. That's what my mother used to say to me, and it's still good advice."

"Do you really think I could manage thi—"

The door was opened by Susan; her hands were empty. Selina glared at her, but Susan ignored the glare and said, "Beg pardon, but there's a gentleman named Vogel in the living room. To see Mr. Felix."

Felix, gray-faced under his tan, groaned. "The police lieutenant!" Laura turned pale and put down her soup spoon.

Selina ordered crisply, "Tell him to wait."

Susan nodded, gave a half-curtsey and left the room. Felix pushed back his chair, but Selina motioned sharply at him to stay in his place.

"If he wants to see you that's his problem," she said. "We're eating, and this is our home."

Felix glanced from his mother to Laura, then to the door and back to the table, obviously weighing trouble with his mother against every other problem he had to deal with.

Selina finally broke the awkward silence by turning to Jack and saying in a more normal voice, "Tell us one of your stories about those sheiks—and make it a funny one."

Jack was obliging her with a long, contrived anecdote when a soft rap sounded on the door. He paused momentarily, and Selina whirled around furiously as the door opened.

Lieutenant Vogel stood outlined against the bright light of the hallway. He worked the palm of a hand along the top of his bullet head as he stepped into the room. He looked sharper and more alert than he had earlier in the day, and he seemed perfectly at ease. He was jacketless, with a white shirt and a somewhat askew tie. Except for a certain military stiffness, he might have been at home.

"I suppose you didn't get the message that I was here," he said, directing his query to Felix and Laura. "I promised to let you know personally about the autopsy report, and that's what I came to do."

Selina interrupted angrily. "Introduce me, Felix, to this stranger in our dining room."

"Mother, this is Lieutenant Vogel of the local police force."

"Are you aware," Selina said, drawing herself up regally, "that you've chosen to interrupt a private family dinner and charge in as though this was a den of criminals?"

"I'm here to keep a promise, ma'am—and to give your son a warning."

"My son needs no warnings from the likes of you," Selina said coldly. "Your impertinence will be reported, I can assure you, to a higher authority in the police force."

"One of the reasons I'm here, ma'am, is that a higher authority told me to come here instead of forcing your son and daughter-in-law back down to headquarters."

"Were you instructed to behave so rudely?"

"Ma'am," Vogel said patiently. "I've put in a hard day's work today, and all I want to do is to go home as soon as possible, eat a decent meal, watch TV for a few hours, and get some rest. I don't intend to be kept cooling my heels until *somebody* sees fit to grant me an audience."

"Your personal desires are of no interest to me," Selina snapped, turning away.

A steely glint appeared in Vogel's sharp eyes.

Laura intervened. "Suppose Felix and the lieutenant go into the sitting room to have some coffee and discuss this."

"No!" Selina gestured to her maid at the door. "Susan, As soon as you're through here, I want you to telephone Mr. Gayley, our attorney, and ask him to come over to Coralton as soon as possible."

Susan nodded and withdrew swiftly.

Vogel stood against the wall, not far from the Vermeer painting that Laura had grown to admire. He made a point of leaning one shoulder against the wall and crossing his legs, as if he was prepared to wait all night if necessary.

Laura addressed Vogel directly. "Are you here to put my husband or myself under arrest?"

Vogel shook his head. "No, ma'am."

"Do you intend to ask us any more questions?"

"Not tonight," Vogel said. "We covered that ground pretty carefully when you and Mr. Page were in my office last night and earlier this morning."

"And *we* didn't have to wait at all," Laura gently reminded him.

Felix stood up as she finished. "Let's go into another room, Vogel, and get this over with."

His mother's voice rang out. "I have sent for Mr. Gayley, our attorney, to join you. I suggest you wait for him...."

It was Jack who broke in quietly. "If that's *Ted* Gayley you're talking about, Selina—and I suppose it is—he couldn't stop the lieutenant from pulling a fast one if he tried. I know Ted pretty well. He's a corporate lawyer, one of the best, but he knows as much about criminal law as he knows about putting up one of the office buildings Felix designs."

Felix continued on his way through the door with Jack's words ringing in his ears. By the time Noland had finished his thought, it was too late for the older woman to interfere when she realized that her son already had left the room.

At the door, Vogel turned and caught Laura's eye.

"Won't you join us, too, please?" he asked politely. "For the sake of completeness, you might say."

Laura jumped up from her seat in her rush to join her husband.

Vogel added lightly as she joined him, "And to keep you from sitting on pins and needles, of course."

She said gratefully, "Thank you very much, Lieutenant."

Selina managed to give one additional order. "Use the West Room," she called out.

Felix obviously heard her request because he led the way reluctantly into the West Room. Neither he nor Laura felt especially comfortable there. It was much too elaborate to suit either of them.

"This is like a museum," Vogel said, looking around at the furnishing and decorations in open-mouthed admiration. "My wife would give a fortune to even see a place like this."

"You'll have to describe it to her carefully," said Laura, who had begun researching the room's treasures. She was doing her best to return at least one small favor for Vogel's larger one. "The Italian wall painting there goes back to the seventeenth century, I believe. That's a Portuguese cabinet over there with the harp design on each door. Above it is a Louis XV carved panel...."

"I'll try to remember all that to tell my wife," Vogel said gratefully. "She gets after me if I get to see inside an expensive house like this and don't give her a report on .the furnishings afterwards. But worst of all, she's never satisfied with what I tell her. My boss doesn't complain half as much about my work reports as she does about my 'home' reports."

"Well, I have an idea," Laura said. "Once all this nasty business is behind us—and I'm certain it will be—why don't you bring your wife over one afternoon and I'll show her around."

"Why that would be...." Vogel could hardly contain himself. "That would be very kind of you, ma'am...."

From his position in the middle of the room, Felix glowered at the two impatiently: "Well?" he asked the lieutenant. "What was so important that you had to drag us out of our dinner?"

"It doesn't look too good," Vogel answered in a more businesslike voice. "Not from your point of view, I mean."

"Speak your piece."

"Can I sit on one of these chairs? I had a pretty rough day today, and that sort of thing takes it out of a man." Vogel sat down heavily on a small antique side chair, but Laura noticed only that his eyes hadn't left Felix at all. "The bad news is that *no* bullets were found in Oscar Clymer's body or on the bridge—or in the canyon area either. Your story about the gunfire simply doesn't hold up."

While Felix glared silently, Laura asked: "But how did Mr. Clymer die then?"

"His neck was broken."

Laura shuddered, and the memory of Oscar, chuckling gleefully at the rubber ball as he took it out of his pocket on that last walk, loomed painful and vivid before her.

"I assume, then, that it happened when Mr. Clymer fell into the canyon."

"That's what I assume, too, but the conflicting stories you've told make it necessary for the investigation to continue."

"My husband and I have only told one story, and that one happens to be the truth."

"Three shots were fired, and Clymer fell against the bridge railing, so he broke it and dropped into the canyon," Vogel said flatly. "Well, I can't deny at this stage that what you two have said *is* remotely possible. But something else is possible, too, I can think of at least one variation on your story that could make sense but isn't nearly as flattering to Mr. Page."

Laura hoped that Felix would remain in control of his temper.

"We'd like to hear that story, Lieutenant," she said. "That is, if you don't object to telling it."

"Not at all," Vogel said. "In fact, it's a big stumbling block right now, like I just told you. If we knew the right or wrong of it, the case could be solved."

He drew out a slim pipe, glanced affectionately at it and then looked warily at the surroundings. He sighed, shook his head, and put the pipe back in a breast pocket.

"It's simple enough," he went on. "There was *some* noise, presumably, and Clymer lost his balance and toppled over. The two of you ran to the end of the bridge and Mr. Page eased himself down into the canyon to see if anything was wrong with Clymer. Now we know that Clymer had been giving Mr. Page a hard time and that Mr. Page's temper isn't the most accommodating in this world. Seeing his enemy lying there, maybe stunned, it's possible that—"

"No!" Laura called out in order to stop the lieutenant from finishing what he was going to say, but Vogel went on exactly as if there'd been no interruption from her.

"—Mr. Page took advantage of the situation and broke Clymer's neck then and there."

"You're completely wrong, Lieutenant. You couldn't be more wrong."

"Prove it and I'll agree with you."

"My husband's temper only shows itself against people who are confronting him at the moment. Felix would never hurt anybody who was already at a disadvantage."

"That isn't proof," Vogel said. "But we do know that Clymer had been giving your husband a rough time and was in a position to block him from having what he wanted most of all."

"I would think," Laura said coolly, "that your medical examiner could tell the difference between one cause of death and another."

"Doctors aren't miracle men," Vogel remarked, obviously hating to admit that some police jobs couldn't be done to perfection, no matter how hard one tried. "Clymer could have been in bad shape to start with, and Mr. Page gave him the *coup de grâce*—if you know what I mean—the 'finishing touch.'"

"It's nonsense!" Laura snapped.

Felix intervened, a little too loudly. "Just a minute!"

He coughed and cleared his throat when Vogel looked across inquiringly at him.

"Do you ever expect a solution to this death?"

"The medical examiner is going to keep the case open, and he plans to consult with some specialists."

"How long do you suppose it'll take before I'm out from under all blame?"

"Depending on the results, of course," Vogel pursed his lips, "I would say it will be a week or two at the least. The M.E. might need to travel to another area to do his consulting."

Felix rubbed his hands together fiercely in frustration. "And during all this time, everybody in El Norte is going to be under the impression that I was the one who gave Clymer 'the finishing touch,' as you so charmingly phrased it."

"Well, you're not under arrest—and that should be some consolation."

Felix laughed mirthlessly, still clenching and unclenching his fists. "So I will be able to go down to Jacksonville and speak to the Highway Commission people until my tongue turns blue, but coming from a man who may have killed someone over this very issue, it will all amount to nothing. All the same, what other avenue is open to me, except to go there and try to convince them?"

Vogel had been halfway to the door, but he whirled around.

"I'm sorry, Mr. Page, but you won't be going near Jacksonville for the next couple of weeks, at the least."

Felix took a threatening step toward Vogel, but halted before Laura could call out. The two of them stood facing the lieutenant, Laura with a warning hand automatically extended in front of her husband.

"Look. This is simply a matter of routine," Vogel went on. "During any investigation of a suspicious death, all 'persons of interest,' and that certainly includes you two, are required to stay in close proximity to the scene. And there isn't a lawyer anywhere who could change that prohibition. That's the 'sort of' warning I came to give you. And if you're tempted to ignore it, even for a day trip to Jacksonville, consider it as a 'real' warning."

Vogel watched Felix carefully. The younger man's fists were flexing and clenching, almost as if they had a will of their own. He glanced at Laura.

"I still believe your husband is going to get angry at you one of these days, Mrs. Page," he said with a shake of his head. "And he won't be able to control himself."

With his words of warning echoing eerily in the heavily-furnished old room, Vogel turned and stomped out of the room.

CHAPTER ELEVEN

"I'm surprised that the architect wasn't garroted, or whatever else they do to criminals there," Jack was saying smoothly when Laura and Felix rejoined the diners. "This fellow has never been the same, since the authorities complained to him for installing a row of toilets that faced Mecca."

As her son and his wife entered, Selina's smile froze and she thrust her jaw out as if she were stepping vigorously on something nasty underfoot.

"We waited the main course for you," she said accusingly. "Now tell us what happened, Felix."

"Yes," Harvey agreed, and the mask of polite boredom on his face was replaced with one of eager interest. "What did the policeman say?"

Laura stopped herself from suggesting that this conversation not be held until the meal was finished. She realized that there wasn't anything else on Felix's mind, and he'd have a hard time talking about trivial subjects.

"The autopsy results aren't conclusive yet, but the alternative theory, according to Lieutenant Vogel, is that I killed Oscar Clymer by breaking his neck while he was lying unconscious down in the canyon."

Evelyn winced but said easily, "As long as you *aren't* under arrest, I would think that there's no serious trouble."

"The 'trouble' is that everybody in and around El Norte is going to be convinced that I'm a murderer who's loose only because he has money and influence."

"If anybody ever says that, and I'm listening," Harvey said loyally, "I'll jam his teeth down his throat."

"Of course, Harvey. I'm sure you'll overhear some stranger talking about your brother while you're on one of those frequent driving trips you make into Apocalypse." Selina said straight-faced,

Harvey realized that she had made a fantastic joke at his expense, and smiled and nodded in appreciation.

The main course was finally served, and Laura focused on the delicious aroma of roast chicken which permeated the room. She had expected that one of the advantages of her unexpected wealth would be a gradual lessening of the hold such things as the scent of good food might have on her. Apparently, she had been mistaken. Instead, she was reminded distinctly of one of the foster homes in which she had lived—and for a brief moment she *knew* that she was going to be given the wing or neck. But the feeling left her quickly, sped on its way by Jack's smooth, rumbling voice....

"You're not under arrest, Felix, so you should be able to carry on with your business as usual."

"Such as listening to your stories about the Middle East?"

"Accra, in fact," Noland said with a grin. "I was just telling your mother and Harvey about another architect friend of mine, who was hired to put up a hospital there. First off, the government people got sore at him because the building didn't start to go up on the day after the plans were approved. Then they told him they didn't want a building that looked European—Heaven forbid!—or native—no 'quaintness,' even though it might be functional in that climate. Then the bureaucrats wanted a cut of the funds before construction could begin—and the local Communists insisted that the unskilled laborers couldn't learn even the most simple techniques that are necessary in Africa. And after that business with the toilets, some major changes had to be made. Then the government decided that women and men wouldn't be allowed to use the same building, and a lot of persuasion was required to change their thinking on that! Right after that, the government was thrown out of office, and now my friend is still waiting for permission from the new group in power to go ahead with the building."

Selina said. "I know that Felix prefers even the stupidest of clients here to the sort of people he'd have to deal with in wherever-it-is. I'm sure that Felix could never be tempted to go abroad, no matter how much money was involved."

"Mother," Felix smiled grimly at her. "I promise I won't even be going to Jacksonville to make my pitch to the State Commission. At least, not until it's too late."

"You'd be making a hell of a mistake not to go and make your presentation in Jacksonville," Jack said. "At least you can get it on the record."

"Even if I *could* get up the nerve to make my pitch at a public hearing, I still couldn't do it." Felix looked down the table at the faces staring at him. "According to Vogel, Laura and I are not allowed to leave this area until the Clymer case is settled. And God only knows when that will be...."

Selina shook her head. "As soon as I get on the phone to Inspector Butcher, that terrible little man—Vogel—was that his name?—will make no more trouble for you—believe me!"

"Vogel said his superiors were in total agreement with what he was doing." Felix suddenly struck his clenched fists sharply against the table top.

Laura, instinctively, put out her hands to keep Felix from possibly hurting himself, but she couldn't halt the flow of energy and pressure within him. A reddish glow was creeping upwards past the second knuckle of each finger where he had struck it.

In hopes of diverting his thoughts, Laura spoke up encouragingly:

"Darling, I'm sure that this problem *can* be solved, and your not being allowed to go to Jacksonville doesn't finish everything for us."

Felix's fists hit the table top again, viciously. Laura saw that his fists had come down directly on the space in the highly polished surface where her reflected image had been, and she wished she hadn't noticed that.

"You've never really wanted to make a public appeal, Felix," she insisted. "And this way you'll have more time to get things done from here and persuade others around to your—our—way of thinking. The citizens of El Norte can't possibly ignore what you say, Fel—"

Felix suddenly shouted:

"For heaven's sake, Laura, *shut up*!"

Laura fell back as if she had been assaulted, remembering in spite of herself that Lieutenant Vogel had just been warning her about Felix's bad temper.

"I'm sick of being blocked on all sides," Felix added bitterly. "And on top of everything else, my dear wife tells me that it's all fine and dandy."

Laura started to object: "I never said that, Felix," she insisted softly.

"Do you believe that the police aren't in cahoots with the vultures determined to take this land over? Do you suppose that Gordon isn't putting pressure on them to keep me from the hearing—now that there's a convenient excuse?"

From what seemed like a long distance, she heard Jack's soothing voice. "Felix, you're a long-time friend of mine; but I've been on good terms with Gordon for some years now too, and I can't believe he'd do anything like that. I'm not sure if he even wants to go through with this business about putting up houses in El Norte, especially after what's happened to Clymer, but I certainly can't see him being as underhanded as you seem to think...."

Felix jumped up from his seat. "Then why don't *you* go tell him that? This is the final straw for me, to invite a so-called friend to dinner then have to sit here and listen to him making excuses for the likes of Gordon Ulric."

Noland said, "I'm sure we can settle this in a reasonable way, Felix. Sit down and let's not lose our heads."

"To hell with both you and Gordon Ulric!"

Felix glared ferociously across the table at Noland. Laura

stood up and faced him with a gentle but firm smile on her lips.

"Felix. We need to be calm about something as important to all of us as—"

She suddenly felt what seemed like an explosion erupting against her left cheek. Her head bounced over toward her right shoulder, as if it belonged to a rag doll, and she felt for a moment as if *she* were the rubber ball that Oscar Clymer had been squeezing in his hand—shortly before his violent death. Shortly before his neck had been broken—Lieutenant Vogel had insisted—by a pair of human hands. But she'd never believe that of Felix. Never....

The side of her face stung as she raised her head. Tears rose unbidden against her trembling eyelids and lingered on their fragile perch.

Jack and Evelyn looked at each other in the manner of long-wed people who understand one another's thoughts without having to talk about them.

A chair scraped back against the floor from the other side of the table. Jack Noland stood and said with a tinge of regret:

"Selina, I'm afraid that Evelyn and I will have to be going. You'll excuse us, I'm sure...."

"I'm so sorry you have to leave early." Selina spoke the polite words automatically, her right hand groping for the crook of her cane.

"One other thing, Selina. Please inform your son," he pointedly avoided Felix's glare, "that I had been about to volunteer my own time to go down to that committee hearing in Jacksonville and put his plans before it. And, if I'm not mistaken, I think I could have been pretty damn persuasive."

The statement brought Laura up short. She understood that Jack would have taken Felix's place as well as was humanly possible.

"You still must do it!" she said, pleading with her eyes.

Harvey suddenly laughed as if all the tension had left the dining room. "Yes, Jack. That's a wonderful idea! I'll bet you could talk an Indian into giving up his feathers. We're all set,

Jack. You're going to Jacksonville, and you and Felix are friends again." He glanced hopefully at his brother.

"Things don't always work out so easily, Harvey" Jack said gently. "I'm not going to any of the hearings at all—now."

Laura wouldn't give up, "But you live in El Norte, too, just like we do. If you let these developers take over, you'll be living in the same difficult conditions as we will."

"That's true, Laura," Jack conceded, "but after spending a little time with your husband, in this 'generous and forgiving' mood of his, I've simply stopped caring about all that."

Felix pounded the table top again, but refrained from shouting at Noland to leave his house.

Jack and his wife, ignoring Felix's outburst, made a further point of thanking Selina for her hospitality, of telling Laura how glad they were to meet her, and of commenting that Harvey looked better than ever. They made their way out deliberately and with unhurried steps. Just as if nothing had gone wrong, and they had enjoyed a pleasant evening and dinner with friends.

Harvey broke the silence that followed their guests' departure by saying cheerfully, "I hope we'll see them again soon. Jack is a very funny guy, a *real* joker—not like that phony Clymer fellow."

"Be quiet, Harvey," Selina said.

Laura didn't realize how much of a strain the evening had been for her until she was alone again with just the family. Her breathing was harsh and irregular. She knew it would be unwise to confront Felix in front of the others, so she said her good-nights quietly and left the room.

Harvey, overlooking his mother's earlier admonishment, called out to Laura as she reached the door:

"Why don't you two lovebirds stop being so unfriendly and kiss and make up?"

"Harvey!" Selina thundered. "I said to be quiet!"

Laura shut the door firmly on them without comment and sought the relative peace and quiet of her bedroom.

CHAPTER TWELVE

Laura gathered up her pajamas, bathrobe, and toiletries, and carried them to the bedroom she had originally used when Felix first brought her to Coralton, the one with the crazy round bed. She had disliked that bed from the start; she preferred one of the conventional types with the longer side placed up against a wall. In fact she had slept against a wall since childhood, telling herself, when she was very young, that nobody was ever going to push her through that wall to the other side.

She had willed herself to stop dwelling on what had happened earlier in the evening, but she could not hold to her resolution for very long. If it were not for the problem of transportation, she would have gone to the hotel in Apocalypse, provided she would have been able to leave the house without Selina's knowledge.

Felix's mother had probably given her son orders to stay away from Laura for the night, to let her stew in her own juices. And she had probably tried to convince Felix to accept, at last, that Laura was an undependable girl with no true sense of family, and with no feeling for the continuity of Coralton's traditions or those of El Norte.

So Laura had resigned herself with some relief to a quiet night, and it was disturbing, then, to hear a series of hesitant raps at the door.

"Felix?"

Laura opened the door to him. He obviously had been drinking to get up his courage to talk to her. The top button of his shirt had popped open, and his tie was askew. He entered awkwardly and looked away from Laura, in spite of the fact that he had come to talk to her. The hard chair he chose creaked when he sat down on it with a thud.

"Well, Laura?" he asked. "Let me hear it."

"There's nothing I want to say."

"Don't you even want to tell me that you hate me, or that I'm no good? Don't you want to get all that over with?"

Laura realized that this was just the sort of reproach he might have expected from Selina during a conflict of wills. She glanced at him in pity, but he was gazing intently at a point away from her, and didn't see her face.

"I *don't* hate you, Felix, and I don't think you're evil either, for that matter."

"What then?" He looked at her in disbelief. "Are you going to suffer in silence? Are you one of those women who won't speak at all when she's angry?"

"When I'm mad, Felix, I get mad as hell. And I work it out of my system by shouting—not through violence."

"All right, I deserved that."

"I wasn't trying to needle you, Felix. I was just stating a fact."

He thought quietly a moment then said, "I should have brought you a gift, to make it up to you. But there are no stores nearby. And a gift wouldn't really change anything. Would it? I got so mad I could hardly talk and, God help me, I slapped you. It was the last thing in the world I intended to do, but I just couldn't seem to stop myself. This whole El Norte business has brought out my worst side, and I strike out at anyone who dares to stand in my way. I swear to you I've never done anything this bad before, and hopefully it won't ever happen again. But it *did* happen. And I'm appalled by it."

"And it *will* go on happening," Laura said. "I know it will—if we have any more disagreements about your part in keeping El Norte intact."

"Laura, I won't let myself touch you again—not that way."

"But can you stop it?"

"Of course, I—" He looked down at his hands and shook his head. "I'll do my best to make sure it never happens again."

"I know you will, Felix." Laura agreed. "I just don't think that 'your best' is likely to be particularly effective, given your present state of mind."

"Look, Laura. I've got a request to make. I didn't want to suggest this, but for your sake I must. I think you should move out of the house for a few weeks—take a room at the Apocalypse Hotel and wait until this business about El Norte is settled, once and for all. I know it won't be much longer. There has to be some decision from the State Commission very soon. We can see how the wind is blowing at that point—and take the proper steps afterwards."

He paused, eyes cast down. Laura knew what it had cost him to make a suggestion like that. For her to leave him, even for a short time, would be a public admission that he was not a stable man emotionally—and that she was afraid of him. Further, it would be a confirmation of sorts to Felix as well. That kind of knowledge could push a man toward the edge of his endurance.

"No," she said decisively. "I won't go along with that idea."

"You mean you don't want—" He swallowed hastily. "Do you mean then that you want a divorce immediately?"

"Certainly not. You misunderstand me."

His eyes burrowed into hers in anguish and confusion—and just a trace of hope.

"If I walked out on you now, during this crisis, I'd be a very poor wife, indeed," she continued. "And you would deserve to divorce me, Felix."

"I see," he said. "You mean you want us to stay under the same roof, but apart."

"For tonight, at least," she said. "I think I deserve to be on my own for a few more hours...."

He stood up quickly and turned to go, not wishing to intrude on her privacy for another moment. He was so anxious to oblige her, in fact, that he stopped in shock when Laura spoke:

"Good night, *dear.*"

"Oh!" He looked back at her, shamefaced, then hesitated and said, "Good night, dearest one. Bless you and sleep well."

He closed the door softly behind him.

Laura cried herself to sleep that night, not for the first time, nor, did she suppose, for the last.

* * * * * * *

Sunday passed without further event. There was the visit to El Norte's old church, where she felt the eyes of a number of people looking her up and down. There were the short talks, later on, with many near-strangers, whom she had met only once or twice. There was the awkwardness of leaving church so as to avoid bumping into Gordon and his lovely red-haired daughter, Janice—the girl whom Felix had been expected to marry.

And then came the long drowsy afternoon in which Laura sat around listlessly while Selina, needles clacking furiously, knitted away on an endless shawl. She stopped knitting just long enough to draft a furious letter to the editor of the *El Norte Beacon* about a recent editorial which disagreed with her point of view. "Tell the truth," she admonished him, on the assumption that her opinion was the only possibility.

Felix and his attorney had gone into Apocalypse, hoping to persuade Lieutenant Vogel and his superiors to allow Felix to make the trip to Jacksonville for his appearance in front of the State Highway Commission. Felix didn't say much, preferring to let his attorney do the talking—so he had only himself to blame when their discussions with the authorities produced no positive results.

Harvey had taken one look at the dismal faces surrounding him and descended to the basement for another afternoon of tinkering with his contraptions. Only when he had mentioned it casually, did Laura become aware that he already had several patents in his name for minor, but mildly profitable, devices of one kind and another.

And dinner would have been impossible if it were not for

Harvey, who went on and on about the stereo set he was putting together during his sessions in the cellar. Felix asked enough questions to keep his half-brother talking incessantly, as he explained the finer points of his mechanical discoveries. Laura, toying with her food, watched him carefully, as he expounded on his various inventions, a thoughtful expression on her face.

Selina, driven by the handyman, left Coralton in the early evening to attend a fund-raising committee meeting in town. The committee's purpose was to raise money to plant shade trees along the main street of Apocalypse, near the hotel. Laura would have appreciated it if her mother-in-law had asked her to join the group, but conceded to herself that she probably would have turned down the invitation.

Later that evening she moved her things back into the room she shared with Felix, and felt relieved to be with him again.

But by Monday afternoon, something happened which caused the situation to take a distinct change for the worse.

Promptly at half-past eleven each morning, a postal delivery truck drove up to the main entrance of Coralton and the day's mail was handed over to Susan who, in turn, carried the bundle to Felix's office. Felix would then sort through the mail, discarding ads or unwanted materials, and holding out business correspondence or bills to be paid. Mail for family members was clipped together and deposited on a silver tray on a small table near the entryway so that each individual could then retrieve his or her own mail. That had been the routine, day in and day out, for as long as Felix could remember. Indeed, he could recall his father punishing him brutally for disturbing the family's mail on the hall table when he was a child.

"But when Harvey did it, he was let off with a slap on the hand," Felix told Laura. "My father was easier on Harvey and I always assumed it was because his own father was dead."

On this particular morning, the routine was followed as usual. Laura was practicing tennis volleys on the family's clay court in the lush yards behind the house. The exercise gave her a chance to work off some tension as well as improve her skill.

Harvey had promised to play with her later on so that she'd be able to judge how much she had accomplished at this session.

Just as she was putting the tennis balls back into their long narrow can, she heard someone running across the grounds in her direction. She stopped and pushed the wayward tendrils of damp blonde hair back in place.

She looked up to see Felix headed directly toward her at full speed. Harvey galloped awkwardly along behind him. Their dress shoes clattered eerily on the hard surface of the court and Felix appeared to be waving a piece of paper in his hand. His face was a deeper shade of red than it should have been, warning Laura that something had happened to upset him—once again!

"This," he gasped, pushing the paper at her. "For you. Just came...."

"You didn't have to run all the way out here with it, did you?"

"He wanted to," Harvey said. He stood, uncomfortably, off to one side.

She took the letter from Felix, but looked at her husband's face quizzically while doing so. Felix, jaw set, appeared to trying to force himself under control.

"I thought it was addressed to 'Mr.' Page," he explained, "so I opened it. When I looked at the envelope again I saw that the letter 's' had been written after the 'Mr' but it was too faint. I don't think I'd have read much more of it, the letter I mean, but I recognized the stationery—and Gordon's handwriting."

"Gordon couldn't possibly be writing to me!" Laura said, puzzled. "Could it be meant for your mother?"

"Why don't you see what he says?" Felix said. *"Or do you know already?"*

These last words seemed to have been forced out against his will. He drew a deep breath and turned away from her, as if to go. It was Harvey this time, who put out a gentle hand to restrain Felix from leaving the tennis court.

The letter wavered in Laura's trembling hands. Gordon's name, engraved in raised script on the top of the customized letter paper, popped out at her. Taking a deep breath she read aloud:

"My Dear Laura:

This is to thank you for the help and support you've provided me in my fight to make El Norte a place where many people can live and to open up its riches and beauty to all those who haven't been so fortunate as to be born here.

I realize that you can help stealthily, only a little at a time, and that Felix must be led to believe that you're still on his side, *encouraging* him to do *exactly the opposite* of what both of us really want. I can only congratulate you on the smoothness with which you've been accomplishing this task. Your skill as an actress has really come into its own here! I pledge to you that your reward will be ample, when finally you see for yourself what a fine area our little stretch of country can become—just as soon as it is more thickly populated.

Janice sends her regards and asks me to convey that she realizes now how much she misjudged you on the night that you two first met....

Sincerely,

Gordon

P.S. I won't put my name on the outside of this envelope for obvious reasons, and I'm hoping that private mail is still treated with respect at Coralton. But still I can't resist sending you my very best personal thanks."

Laura was surprised at how calm she felt as she turned to Felix:
"Do you believe what is in this?"

"To tell you the truth, I don't know what to believe...."

"You might have tried holding off judgment until you asked me for the truth."

"I'm asking you now."

"But you've made up your mind already, haven't you?" Laura let the letter drop from her shaking hand to the hard-baked floor of the court. "There doesn't seem to be any point in discussing the matter rationally; you won't believe me—no matter what I say."

"Laura!" His voice was suddenly not as clear as it had been. A dull flush had appeared at the base of his throat and traveled up, towards his face. His fists were clenched. Harvey huddled nearby, his eyes blinking rapidly in agony and fear.

"All right. I suppose we do have to talk about it." She nodded. "I assume that Evelyn and Jack told Gordon about what happened here on Saturday night. They probably also told him how they felt about it, too. The incident put an idea into Gordon's head, and he wrote that—that—that lie!"

Felix winced at her mention of Saturday night and glanced down at his right hand—the one that had betrayed him on that fateful evening.

"What's that got to do with it?" he demanded. "I mean, the thing that happened during dinner."

"Gordon probably is hoping that if he can split us up, the emotional pressure will take your mind off what he plans to do here in El Norte."

"There you are! That's probably the truth. It explains everything!" Harvey said in relief.

"But the letter *is* here and I only opened it by accident. How do you explain that?"

"I'm sure you were *meant* to open it," Laura said quietly, "The envelope was written so that you'd misinterpret what it said, and on stationery and in handwriting that's very familiar to you."

"I think this letter proves, beyond a doubt, that when you tried to keep me from getting worried about not going to

Jacksonville," Felix countered, "you were doing exactly what Gordon wanted you to do."

"But I *wanted* you to go—oh, Felix, don't you see? Gordon is trying to get rid of his opposition by breaking us apart."

Felix pounded his hands dully against his thighs. "Laura, all I really know is that this sort of thing mustn't continue. For the sake of my health and yours as well, we can't go on like this!"

"I'm not suggesting that you either believe or disbelieve what was written by your sworn enemy," Laura responded hotly.

"Laura," he said, "What I'm saying is that you've got to get away from here."

"Why? What are you talking about?"

"For *my* piece of mind and your well-being, surely you see you must go. Maybe not for long—or—maybe we really are wrong for each other, and we'll decide it ought to be a permanent separation. You'd certainly have no trouble getting a divorce—and I promise you I wouldn't contest it."

"That's a very easy way to solve a problem," Laura said. "Your temper has gotten the best of you—so get a divorce—and remarry into your proper 'station,' which, I think, is what it used to be called. Somebody like Janice Ulric, I suppose, who was raised with the same privileged background. And if her father should give you a wedding present of the land he currently plans to build on, why, that wouldn't be too bad an outcome, either, *would it?*"

Felix whirled away from her, his hands extended in front of him and curled like claws. If he had stayed facing Laura, he probably would have done violence to her again, and each of them knew it. Harvey, watching their escalating argument with wide and wounded eyes, whimpered softly to himself.

"You didn't have to turn away from me just then," Laura said, her voice sinking to a whisper. "If someone else had been saying those things, you'd have attacked first and felt sorry about it later, if at all. But even though I provoked you to the limit, Felix, and I admit I did it on purpose to find out what you'd do this time, *you didn't touch me!*"

"Laura," he said. This time his soft voice matched hers. "I think you can see that it's safer for you if you leave."

"But you don't really want me to go, do you?" she asked. "If you did, you'd have tried to get rid of me with those hands of yours—or you'd have thrown me out of Coralton a long time ago. Felix, I believe we need each other very much now, and I'd like you to confirm that for me."

"For your own sake...," he began. He might have been talking to her from the moon. "I'll be honest with you. I don't know how long I can control myself if this sort of thing keeps happening."

"You'll have to begin to learn how," Laura said firmly. She knew her face had turned pale with the strain of their confrontation, but she was determined to resolve this, once and for all. "The two of us will never need each other more than we do now, at this moment, and I refuse to leave you, just as long as I can draw breath."

PART THREE

CHAPTER THIRTEEN

Laura walked back through the house with her head held high. Not until she was more than halfway to her destination did she realize that she subconsciously had drawn up her left hand to protect her throat. She thrust her hand down to her side instantly, and was grateful that no one had been close enough to see what she'd been doing.

Lightly, and taking care to exhibit no signs of tension, she made her way toward the bedroom—the one that she and Felix shared. As she walked down the hall, she saw that their door was standing open. The vacuum-cleaner was not humming away, as she half expected; instead, she heard the silky rustle of clothing being folded.

Laura stood on the threshold and looked in. A ray of sun from the window illuminated Susan's shiny uniform and the expensive leather suitcase lying open on the bed. The maid was placing precisely ordered suits and dresses carefully into the bag as Laura watched from the door.

"Why are you packing my things?" Laura demanded.

Susan spun around, and Laura could see the lines of concern that etched her normally calm face.

"We're all so sorry about what's happened, ma'am...," she began.

Laura waited, not trusting herself to ask the question.

"Mrs. Page told me about it, ma'am," Susan continued uncertainly. "She said you were leaving for a while, and that's all she said. But I could tell from her voice what had *really* happened, and I'm so sorry."

"Just when did Selina tell you this?"

"Just before I came up here, ma'am. She was talking to Mr. Felix and he went running out of the house with a letter in his hand. Mrs. Page looked very—well, satisfied—in a grim sort of way. Like she had just found out something important. Not that she takes pleasure in other people's troubles, don't you know, but she does want to have her own way about things."

"Yes. I've noticed that as well," Laura said thoughtfully. "Where is Selina now, do you know?"

"In the summer room, I should think. At least that's where she was when she called me in and told me to pack your things for you."

Laura didn't bother to ask any further questions, but rushed downstairs and to the main wing of Coralton. She was still wearing her tennis outfit and she wished she'd had time to shower and change before she had this necessary conversation with the older woman. A suit of armor, perhaps, she thought grimly. Something that would protect her from head to toe.

Selina was seated at one of the writing tables in the summer room, planning the week's dinner menus. As Laura silently entered the room behind her, Selina scratched out a line, then shook her head and murmured to herself:

"Felix enjoys scampi, so that's what we'll have...and that'll be...."

Laura cleared her throat and spoke loudly:

"Selina, may I talk to you?—Now?"

Selina looked up from her notepad in surprise. She extended her hand for the crook of her cane and raised it carefully from the table. Her gray hair glittered with the movement.

"I should think that you'd go out of your way to avoid talking to me."

"Are you willing to give me a few minutes of your time?" Laura persisted.

"Very well, if you like."

Selina's pointless graciousness reminded Laura of one of

her former directors. Shortly after a particular actor had been fired and no longer presented any kind threat to the director's authority, there was no longer any need for him to be treated with anything but courtesy.

In Selina's case, though, that situation was going to change in a very short time.

"When I went to my bedroom just a moment ago," Laura said, "I found Susan packing my clothes. She told me that she'd been given those orders by you."

"That's correct."

"What gave you the right to order Susan to pack my things?"

"Well...." Selina hesitated. "I had been speaking to Felix earlier and he told me about a disturbing letter you had received. He said that the letter was the last straw so far as he was concerned, and that he was prepared to send you away. It seemed to me that in order to make your situation a little easier, I could instruct Susan to attend to your packing. I realize that packing suitcases is a highly individual affair by and large," she rattled on, oblivious to Laura's glare, "but Susan is quite good at it, and I did want to spare you the embarrassment of being at Coralton any longer than—ah, necessary."

"There *is* no embarrassment," Laura said clearly and sharply, "because I have no intention of leaving!"

Selina's face turned ashen. "I'm sure I've misunderstood you."

"I'm sure you haven't," Laura smiled warmly, as if she was extremely pleased at being the bearer of such good news. "I won't be leaving my husband, Selina, now or ever!"

The color of Selina's face didn't change, and the chiseled patrician features which Felix had inherited, seemed to grow even sharper. The tip of her pointed nose twitched savagely.

"But surely you *can't* mean to stay!"

"The only way you'll get me out of here is by force," Laura stated bluntly.

"I'm not above using force for my son's sake," Selina responded coldly.

"Are you absolutely certain that's what *he* wants?" Laura asked, this time in a softer tone.

Selina rapped the crook of her cane against the table top in frustration. "There is no sense to all to this conversation about nothing. You have to leave, now."

Laura didn't bother to repeat what she'd already told her mother-in-law, but went on reasonably:

"Now I have left Susan upstairs still packing, I was in such a hurry to see you and straighten things out between us. So I must get back and give her new orders."

Selina opened her mouth as if to respond to this insubordination, but clapped it shut instead.

Laura went on: "One of your servants will probably learn what happened between us, and she'll tell all the others, no doubt. I suppose it will be a juicy bit of gossip for them, wouldn't you say?"

"My servants aren't allowed to gossip," the older woman said waspishly.

"All the same, it would be nice if we could find a happy way out of this...difficulty," Laura said. "For instance, *you* could call Susan down and pretend that you've talked me into staying and rescind your original order. That ought to do the trick."

"I refuse to be any part of such a 'theatrical' stunt," Selina sniffed. "*I'm* not a stage actress."

"No, but if you do this one thing you'll save yourself a certain amount of embarrassment...later."

Selina gripped the cane even tighter. She stood up slowly and walked over to the house phone against the farthest wall. Before picking it up, she gave a grim nod and looked across at Laura. "You, my girl" she said, "are wickedly clever!"

Laura was tired but relieved when she entered the Spanish salon just before dinner. After solving the suitcase dilemma, she had given herself the luxury of spending the afternoon browsing through furniture catalogs and making some notes, as well as talking to Mrs. Myers, the cook, about Felix's favorite dishes and writing down the recipes.

She had been chatting quietly about nothing important with Selina and Harvey for only a few minutes when Susan entered with an envelope on a tray and took it straight to Laura. Susan seemed puzzled over her afternoon's useless work of packing and unpacking; but it was not in her nature to be resentful, and she spoke with her customary cheerfulness.

"Mr. Felix asked me to deliver this note to you, ma'am, before dinner."

"Thank you, Susan."

Laura opened the note cautiously and took in what was penned on the stiff stationery without quite registering the full meaning of the words. It suddenly occurred to her what an important part letters seemed to playing in her life today.

Harvey spoke up hopefully, "Good news, I hope?"

"No, actually, I'm afraid it's not." She looked directly at her mother-in-law. "It says, 'Laura, I've decided to stay in town for the time being since I believe it's necessary that we be away from each other for a while. Please don't be angry or upset. But please try to realize that I'm doing this because I care for your well-being—and because I can't yet be sure how much I can trust myself.' Here," she added to Selina. "I think you'd better see the rest of this for yourself."

Laura handed the letter to her mother-in-law and got up and left the room. It gave her no consolation that Selina would now be examining the words above her son's signatures: *"All my love, always."*

CHAPTER FOURTEEN

For the second time since her marriage, Laura slept alone. She had gone directly upstairs with a book and a few chores in mind. The evening passed in doing them, and not for the first time, she thanked heaven silently that such necessities kept one from thinking too much.

But bed itself was a different matter. She hesitated in front of the phone on the night stand and then brought her right hand hurriedly down to her side. She glared balefully at the phone every so often after that, but the glares changed, in spite of herself, to pleading looks.

By ten o'clock, Laura had settled in with a current bestseller. She had finished reading two chapters which took place among animals the author chose to refer to as human beings. She put the book down, feeling a distinct revulsion toward a man who could bring himself to write so unfeelingly about women (probably a married man with a shrewish wife); and for the hundredth time, looked at the telephone on the night table.

She knew she wouldn't be able to get any sleep until she had spoken to her husband, so she placed the call. The clerk at the Apocalypse Hotel told her regretfully that Mr. Page wasn't answering his telephone, which probably meant that he was out of his room. Laura left a message asking Felix to call, and broke the connection.

She couldn't do any more reading so she turned off the light and prepared to relax for a while, at least. She wouldn't go to sleep, of course.

But she was in a surprisingly sleepy frame of mind when she realized that she'd heard a metallic clicking not too far from her.

She stirred and opened her eyes. The big window was closed and a blind moved slightly in the dimness. The cooling system was on, and it made a slight scratchy noise.

Laura turned in bed, automatically looking toward the door. She wasn't surprised, somehow, to see a wedge of light from the hall grow large and then diminish quickly. There was another click of noise as the tongue of the door found its slot.

"Hello, dear," Laura said sleepily. "Wait, I'll put on the light for you."

The newcomer mumbled something or other, and Laura identified it as a request to keep the room in darkness.

"You shouldn't be so darn considerate, Felix," she said. "You'll stumble and fall over something, and it won't really have been any help at all."

The newcomer mumbled again, and Laura knew that he was closer to her. She felt comforted by his presence, but at the same time, and without knowing why, a sense of chilling dismay seemed to start at the top of her throat and work downward.

"Do you realize what's happening to us, dear?" she asked. "You're being extra considerate, and so am I. That can't last. Eventually the honeymoon has to end, and then we'll find out who we really are. Both of us may be in for some surprises, I think."

The newcomer grunted. It was odd, come right down to it, she thought, that Felix hadn't spoken a word to her since he'd walked in.

The newcomer took a careful step that made the floor creak. It seemed odd to her that Felix, who was terribly fastidious, didn't even bother to take off his clothes and brush his teeth before joining her.

Laura's sight was beginning to clear and she could dimly make out the man's figure. He seemed a little broader than she expected, a little heavier. She was going to tell Felix that marriage was making him expand when he suddenly moved toward her.

Perhaps it was supposed to be a playful lunge, but there seemed to be considerable energy in back of it. The upper half of his body would have struck the bed if a pair of hard hands hadn't suddenly been extended against the mattress.

Laura laughed as he straightened up.

"Better luck next time, dea—" she started to say as the phone rang.

The phone rang. It had to be Felix!

It needed only a few seconds for her to understand what had happened. The man in this room with her was a stranger. That playful lunge of his hadn't been intended to be at all playful.

For a longer time than she could have expected she lay paralyzed, terribly aware of her small stature and weak hands. Nothing could be done, absolutely nothing. It would make no sense for her to pick up the phone, either; Felix was too far away to help.

The window was closed. Between her and the door stood this man who had come into her room.

Only afterwards did she realize that the ringing phone had startled him, too. He couldn't possibly have expected it, and there had seemed to be nothing to stop him.

Laura screamed. Her mouth was open and the sound was leaving it before she could do anything else; it was almost as if the sound was in control of her, rather than the other way around.

The stranger's hand was outstretched as he leaned forward, probably to slap her into silence. Laura made claws of her hands and held them at eye level to defend her self.

The man struck out towards her.

Laura felt a piece of cloth suddenly shred against her sharp nails. The newcomer drew back, grunting.

He called out and ran from the bed. The outer door opened and shut loudly. Laura flicked the bed light on, then got up and ran to the door. She locked it and tested it three times to make sure that it would remain locked.

The phone was still ringing; but as Laura hurried toward it so anxiously, it stopped.

She picked it up and phoned the Apocalypse Hotel again, but was told that Mr. Page hadn't returned. Felix must have called independently of her first try to reach him at the hotel.

It was ten forty-five when Laura put through her final call that evening—to Lieutenant Charles Vogel of the Apocalypse police force.

* * * * * * *

"This man was in your room and tried to hit you, but you ripped off a piece of material from the sleeve of his jacket," Lieutenant Vogel said. "And you claim that it wasn't your husband?"

"Of course it wasn't Felix!"

The lieutenant scratched some of the graying hairs at the sides of his head. Laura was sitting with him in the summer room, which was sketchily lit at night. Selina had been excluded after some angry discussion, and Harvey, puzzled and anxious, had gone away reluctantly as well, saying that if Laura wanted any help she should call out for him.

Vogel rubbed his hands against each other. He had come out from his home; the top button of his shirt was undone, his hair was in disarray, and his sports jacket looked as if it had been left out in the elements too long. He frowned down at his notebook as he sat opposite Laura and asked more questions.

"Hadn't your husband made some threats against you in the recent past, and isn't it possible that he might have wanted to carry them out tonight?"

"No, it's not."

"Please explain that."

"My husband will get angry all of a sudden and hit out, but when the storm passes he's perfectly all right. He wouldn't come skulking into the bedroom late at night and try to do me any harm."

"But I assume you know that stories have been going around to the effect that the two of you aren't getting along well." Vogel paused. "One of my jobs is to listen carefully when somebody gossips."

"Then I take it for granted, Lieutenant Vogel, that you know Mr. Page has decided to stay in town for a few days."

"He's only sleeping in town," Vogel said, "but I'm sure he's still trying to get across his ideas about keeping this particular stretch of land the way it was back in the nineteenth century."

Laura said stiffly, "I assume that you aren't too sympathetic to his goals, Lieutenant."

"Well, if your husband loses out, it'll give me fewer policing problems," Vogel said, picking his words carefully. "But he's fighting the tide. The countryside has to change along with everything else in the world, and attempts to keep things as the same always seem to end up being a little foolish."

"Then I take it you'll be buying an apartment in El Norte when Gordon Ulric starts putting up the first of his new projects."

"Does your husband really believe that Ulric could ever get permission—?" Vogel started. "But I suppose Page is running scared, and that adds to my problems. Wait here for me, will you?"

Vogel folded his notebook and walked out of the room, closing the door gently behind him. Laura sat gazing out at the brightly-lit gardens that glowed in the moonlight. Would it be possible, she wondered, in some future Eden, to just sit and do nothing and not have a single worry about Felix enter her head? For a few minutes at least, if luck was with her, she might be so blessed.

Vogel returned more swiftly than she expected. He hesitated longingly in front of the chair he had occupied earlier, but remained standing instead, looking down at her, his face wiped clean of all emotion.

"I'm going to suggest to you that your husband came into your bedroom uninvited and attempted to strike you. In the process of defending yourself, you accidentally snagged and tore the sleeve of his jacket."

"It isn't true!"

"Frankly, I'm beginning to believe that the man is too dangerous to be left out on his own," Vogel continued, ignoring her outburst. "Heaven knows what a man with his hair-trigger temper is likely to do next."

"If my husband loses his temper, it will be because someone has pushed him too far," Laura said. "What's more, he is registered at the Apocalypse Hotel for the time being—and I know he tried to phone me from there tonight, at the precise moment of the attack I reported to you. He couldn't have done it...."

"Your husband hasn't got an alibi—as far as we can tell right now."

"But he must have been in town when he called me!"

"No, he was more likely to be—well, someplace else." Vogel smiled without enjoyment. "I need more work like I need a broken leg, but I'm going to find him and pick him up for questioning."

"And I'm coming with you," Laura said automatically.

Vogel's eyes probed her as if for the first time. "I think you'll be more sensible when you see some actual proof against him—something that not even you will be able to deny."

"There won't be any such proof against him," Laura said with a confidence she didn't really feel.

"No? Well, I just talked to your maid, to your mother-in-law, and to his half-brother. All of them seem to think that the material that you tore off the sleeve of your attacker resembles that of a sports jacket belonging to your husband."

"Then there's more than one jacket like it in the area—and someone else was wearing it tonight! I'm sure of it!"

"You can find out for yourself," Vogel said. "Come with me—and you'd better put on a coat. You're going to need it in this weather...."

"And of course you're going to prevent me from getting in touch with Felix, or leaving a message for him."

Vogel nodded gravely. "Of course."

Laura walked ahead of him up to her bedroom where he stationed himself in the doorway and watched Laura pull out a gray woolen topcoat from her closet. She put it on carefully, taking as much time as she dared, hoping against hope that Felix would have left the place where Vogel expected to find him.

"You can button it when you're in the car," Vogel snapped. "Hurry up!"

She nodded and headed out of the room and down the hall on leaden feet. Just then, however, the bedroom phone rang. Laura darted toward it, but Vogel gently but effectively restrained her.

"Won't somebody pick it up downstairs?" he asked.

"No, that's what I've been trying to tell you. That's Felix's special unlisted number—and this is the only outlet for it."

"I wish you had told me that, before!" In an effort to make himself heard above the insistent buzzer, Vogel's voice was unnaturally loud. "Your husband might very well have been calling this number from town, if, of course, there really *was* a phone call during the attack—and not one invented by you to give him an alibi."

"I *haven't* been lying to you, Lieutenant—I swear!" Laura insisted. "If I wanted to be dishonest with you, why on earth would I have reported the incident that happened here tonight?"

"Maybe you thought your screams had been heard and you had to think up a cover story that was close to the truth as a way of explaining it."

"But Felix didn't come here tonight, I tell you"

"And *I'm* telling *you* that we're going to check that out right now," Vogel said. "Come with me...." And without further ado, he hurried her down the hall, down the stairs and out the front door to his car.

Felix's unanswered phone was still ringing shrilly in Laura's brain as they drove down the drive—away from Coralton.

CHAPTER FIFTEEN

Vogel's car was an older model with the fewest possible accessories, a means of transportation intended for work, not pleasure. The motor hummed smoothly enough though, and Laura sat back, gazing through dust-caked windows at El Norte's spectacular landscape. Here was a stretch of land where it might be possible to forget about everything but the earth below and the sky above—and, as Felix had said—about God.

She couldn't help asking Vogel, "Doesn't this expanse of scenery take your breath away?"

But he answered sourly, as she might have expected, "It's hard as hell to protect the residents against outsiders when they live so far from each other and we have to come from as far away as Apocalypse."

"Where are we going?" she asked.

But Vogel didn't respond until he had topped a rise. "There's a public meeting scheduled tonight, one of those 'Let's-pitch-in-and-save-our-land' meetings. I've seen a lot of them in El Norte over the years, but never one with so much urgency behind it. At any rate, there's only one place large enough in El Norte to hold a meeting that's liable to draw so many people."

"The Lunchroom, you mean?"

"Abe Garten's place is more than just a lunchroom, no matter what the locals call it."

"If Gordon Ulric has his way," Laura said evilly, "it'll probably become a nightclub, instead."

She had heard about Abe Garten's Lunchroom, the only business of its kind allowed in El Norte proper. It was a combination grocery, restaurant, and hangout for the locals. Abe let his main room be used for showing movies that met his high standards, or for concerts or other high-class entertainments.

Abe also kept a bulletin board of local events in front of his place. So Vogel was right—if there was going to be any kind of large public meeting going on in El Norte, it was almost certainly being held at Abe Garten's Lunchroom.

The place looked like any other building in the area, except that perhaps forty cars were ringed around it tonight. Vogel unerringly discovered one of the few spaces left, and pulled snugly into it.

Laura followed him up half a dozen wooden steps past the bulletin board and to the entrance.

The bare walls were lined with tables which had been cleared away from the dining area. Two of them had been set up end-to-end near the farthest wall, and Anderton J. Covey, the former U.S. Senator, stood behind them, a gavel in one hand. Perhaps fifty or sixty men, women, and several older teenagers were already seated in the audience. Laura swiftly looked over the crowd and spotted Felix, sitting at the far end of the third row from the front. There were several empty seats in front of him, in back of him, and at his side, as if others had chosen to keep their distance.

Vogel followed Laura's gaze. He whispered, "They must've tried real hard to keep him from hearing about this. Stay here, please."

Ned Boyer, standing near his seat in the middle, was holding forth on some technicality. Vogel made his way down the aisle quickly, took a seat next to Felix and started whispering to him earnestly.

Covey banged the gavel: "Pardon me a moment, Ned...." He looked pointedly at Vogel. "Might I ask you, sir, to refrain from whispering while someone else has the floor? If you wish to speak later, sir, you will be given ample opportunity."

Laura saw Vogel's thumb rise as he gestured toward the

back of the room. Felix stayed where he was, though the thumb rose again. This time more urgently. Felix shook his head with determination.

Laura didn't want to guess what might happen if the two men continued their silent duel. She eased her way down the aisle. An occasional curious glance was directed toward her, and when her identity had been noted, the glances became sharper.

A big, rumpled-looking man suddenly leaned toward her from his seat and introduced himself as Abe Garten. He stated in a loud voice that he guessed she was the one resident of El Norte with whom he wasn't acquainted.

No hands were raised for clarification when Ned finished speaking and took his seat again, but Laura saw Felix move anxiously in his seat and then look around hurriedly. She could guess that he was hesitating about whether or not he could bring himself to speak to this large group, even though he had known most of the people here since childhood.

She sat down in one of the vacant seats in front of Felix and turned to face him. He started at the sight of her, but a glimpse of the chairman kept him from saying a word.

Laura reached out for his comforting hand and drew it towards her. Then she saw it! A two-inch rip on the left sleeve of his light gray sports jacket! She could not take her eyes away from it.

She glanced over quickly at Vogel, and knew immediately that the lieutenant eyes had spotted the rip, too, thanks to her. Laura probably had done her husband more harm in these few minutes than he had done to himself during their whole ordeal.

She squeezed his hand as hard as she could; if he was going to be arrested, there was no way of knowing when she'd get the chance again. Felix called out inadvertently at the sudden pressure of her fingers. The noise was enough to bring the chairman's eyes swiveling around in Felix's direction. Senator Covey's fine features darkened briefly in irritation when he realized who had called out.

"Please ask to be recognized in the usual manner, if you

will," he said. His eyes swept the room. "Is there anyone else who would like to...? Oh, very well then, I call on—ah, you." He gestured in Felix's direction.

Felix pulled his hand away from Laura's grasp and reached into a pocket for a typewritten note which had been folded three times, like a letter. He tried twice to stand, but fell back. His third try was successful. Even so, he teetered back and forth and looked longingly at the seat he'd been occupying.

"Well?" said the chairman. "If you've changed your mind about speaking, we'll get on with other business."

"No, wait!" Felix's voice was raspy and he paused to clear his throat. At his side, Vogel settled back with the air of a man willing to take all night if that will bring him what he wants.

"I'd like to say a few words about—about the buildings that usually go up in old, established neighborhoods such as ours...." He stopped briefly as if wondering how he'd been able to get out even one sentence in front of this large group.

Murmuring broke out toward the back of the audience, but it was stilled frantically by a number of people loudly whispering, "*Shhh!*" Most of the faces emotionless; the onlookers had decided not to be responsive to anything that Felix Page might tell them.

"...changes are being made with no regard to what is already close by," Felix was saying. "A new structure doesn't exist in and for itself, but as part of the neighborhood, the surrounding area. Too many architects forget that simple fact when they put up a one-of-a-kind building, trying to showboat themselves into prominence."

"What has that got to do with *our* situation here?" Covey asked sharply.

Felix warmed to his subject. He insisted that any new structures put up without restrictions were bound to do violence to the concepts under which El Norte had thrived for so many years. He went on to talk about the high points of the program he had drawn up in order to keep El Norte as close to *virgo intacta*—intact—as possible. After giving some consideration to the importance of limiting the width of the Florida Three corridor, he said a few words about expanding, in a controlled way, the existing tourist facilities in and around El Norte.

Laura's eyes wandered from one person to another in the audience, but came back again and again to the face of a matronly woman in the middle who had been knitting industriously throughout Ned's speech, as Laura recalled. But something in Felix's words had caught her attention. She looked up at him, her work temporarily forgotten.

Laura crossed her fingers and told herself not to distract Felix by even a glance of encouragement, or he might lose the thread of his remarks and trail off into vague patches of nonsense.

"Now you've probably heard about plans to fill our scenic sand canyons with earth and to destroy our quaint wooden bridges except one or two for display—and something *has* happened in the last few days which convinces me our bridges can be as dangerous as our opponents claim."

The woman with the knitting nodded slowly and thoughtfully, and Laura saw with satisfaction that her attention had wandered far away from her needlework.

"What I am now suggesting is a compromise," Felix said, "Let's replace the rickety old wooden bridges with concrete-reinforced structures built to visually resemble the old ones as much as possible. Such a move would actually be cheaper than filling in the canyons, and I have spent most of the day working on the facts and figures to prove my point."

The woman with the knitting lowered her eyes at last, nodding. Her needles flashed vigorously. Felix sensed a general consensus of interest and concluded:

"I'll be glad to make my figures available to the chairman— along with my previous report on the entire situation."

Covey looked dazed.

Felix said a brief, "Thank you, all," and sat down. Somebody in the room began to applaud, but was interrupted by the knitting woman's booming voice.

"I'm sure we all deeply appreciate the work that Felix has put in on this," she said, going on to thank him profusely for all he had done, as did several others in the audience.

Felix passed his report forward to the chairman's table. Laura gave him a congratulatory smile and quick kiss then shuddered when she heard Vogel say quietly to Felix:

"All right, Page, you've had your day. You have to face the music now. Come along quietly, or I'll be forced to arrest you in front of all these people."

Felix got to his feet and walked ahead of Vogel toward the door, pausing here and there to accept congratulations for his speech from various members of the group. He had won over a difficult audience, but that glory was over for now. He was about to lose his freedom.

Near the door, the voices of the crowd behind them sounding like the distant drone of an airplane, Felix turned abruptly to the lieutenant.

"Why on earth am I under arrest—now?"

"Let me put it this way to you," Vogel said. "I'm going to give up my evening relaxation, which I need very badly, by the way, in order to ask you some questions. Then *I'll* decide if you're under arrest or not."

"If that's the case you can ask me the questions right here and now."

"I could, but I won't."

Laura looked anxiously at her husband's taut face and said sadly, "I only wish I hadn't taken your hand before you started to talk to those people...."

"What an odd thing to say! What's my hand got to do with anything?" Felix demanded of her. "I wish somebody would tell me once and for all exactly what this is all about."

"I was attacked in our bedroom tonight. A man—at least I think it was a man—tried to hurt me...."

Felix pushed Vogel away from him. "What are you saying? What happened, Laura? Tell me everything."

"I was getting ready to go to sleep and had turned out the light, when someone entered the bedroom. Of course I assumed it was you, and I tried to make a joke of it. Then your private line rang...and...and I knew it had to be *you* on the other end."

"I called twice," Felix pointed at a line of phone booths against the far wall. "From there."

"Can you prove what time you got here? What time you might have placed those calls?" Vogel interrupted.

Felix shook his head. "Go on, Laura. What happened then?"

"I realized the intruder wasn't you and I screamed, and the man, whoever it was, lunged for me...and I tore some material off his jacket, and then he ran out of the room. Then I called Lieutenant Vogel,"

Felix, standing between Vogel and Laura, turned to the lieutenant. "So you came right down here and now you want to ask me more questions. Well, I can't prove what time I got here. Abe must have been in the back somewhere and I didn't speak to him right away. I tried to phone Laura, but there wasn't any answer—and I have no idea what time it was by then. Then I sat alone for awhile in one of the small rooms in the back, going over the figures for the cost of the project I hoped to submit. At some point, I went back to the booth and tried unsuccessfully to reach Laura again. When I came out, people had started to arrive for the meeting. You know the rest...."

Vogel gestured to Felix's left jacket sleeve.

"When did you get that tear in your jacket?"

"Earlier during the day."

"How?"

Felix blinked several times. "Is that the big deal? Laura tore a chunk of material off somebody's sports jacket and you think it was mine. Is that the whole point?"

"*You're* supposed to be answering *my* questions," Vogel said.

Felix turned to Laura. "And do *you* think I was the one who attacked you?"

"I know it *wasn't* you."

"By proof or by feeling?"

"The proof is that I know you."

Then she startled him so that his mouth flew open, as she

suddenly whirled toward Vogel.

"But there *is* proof," she said exultantly. "Real proof that Felix didn't attack me."

"Well, what is it?" Vogel asked.

"The other man used his *right* hand," Laura explained. "His *right* hand. Felix's jacket is ripped on the *left* sleeve. I should have realized it right away, but so many things have been happening that it slipped my mind for a while."

"Your testimony in Mr. Page's favor can't exactly be called courtroom proof."

Laura managed to hide her dismay at Vogel's words as she looked at Felix, but he didn't seem at all worried. He smiled.

"You'll have to prove with scientific evidence, Lieutenant," Felix said, "that the one rip matches the other. I don't believe you can do that."

"And I don't believe in the coincidence of two ripped jackets," Vogel told him.

"But there really *is* a coincidence here." Felix was smiling; this discussion wasn't nearly as painful to him as addressing a large audience; and he'd done well enough at that chore. "Or maybe I can win you over to my side by proving to you that I ripped the sleeve of my jacket someplace else."

"Where?" Vogel asked again. "Show me. Prove it."

Laura heard footsteps behind them and looked around in time to see Gordon approaching them, dressed, as usual, all in black, except for a gleaming white shirt. His hair, gray at the temples, caught an overhead shaft of light as he moved with soldierly stiffness. He spoke only to Vogel.

"I wish you could be quieter over here, Lieutenant," he whispered. "After all, people can see and hear you quite clearly. I can assure you that everyone is disgusted that somebody from El Norte is being placed under arrest." He shot a triumphant glance at Felix, who had turned brick red with anger.

"If I wanted to get someone in trouble and I had a reputation for always dressing in black," Laura said, "I think I'd find a sports jacket to match one belonging to the man I despised and wear it some night—in a dark place—just to see if I could get that man in trouble!"

Gordon looked as if he had suddenly developed a very bad taste in his mouth.

"Mrs. Page," Vogel demanded. "Are you making an official accusation against Mr. Ulric?"

"I'd rather not say any more about that here," Laura said quietly.

Ulric exploded. "This is insane! The woman is desperate to save her husband and will stop at nothing, including putting my reputation in jeopardy to accomplish her goal!"

"Mr. Ulric, I'm inclined to agree with you," Vogel said. "All the same, I'm going to have to ask you to come with me. I think we can better settle this at headquarters."

"I don't intend to be dragged along to the police station like some common criminal."

Vogel smiled. "But that's exactly where you're going, Mr. Ulric," he said. "You can object all you like, but it won't change a thing."

Gordon thought a moment.

"Very well, Lieutenant," he said. "I'll go with you, but I shall ask my daughter to telephone my attorney to meet us there."

"You're entitled to do that, Mr. Ulric, but for the time I can assure you, you aren't seriously suspected of a crime. I only want to ask you a few questions to clear up a few of these matters."

"All the same, I want my lawyer there."

With Vogel's permission he walked back to one of the rear aisles and spoke to Janice, who had been waiting near the end of the row. After a brief whispered consultation, she stood and joined her father in the aisle.

"You shouldn't get the idea, Mrs. Page," Vogel went on, "that the only reason I'm bringing Ulric downtown is because you suggested he might have a part in this. If he has any other dirt on your husband, I expect he'll be sure to bring it up while he's at the station," Vogel turned to Felix. "I think he'll tell us everything he knows about *you*."

"There isn't anything for him to tell," Laura said with a certainty she didn't feel.

"If there *is*, though, I'm going to get it tonight," Vogel said. "I want this case to be solved by morning. I've got too many other things on my plate right now. I need to move on."

"It almost sounds as if I were doing your job for you," Laura said. "But you should know. Ulric can't hurt my husband in any way."

Felix interrupted them. "Just a minute, Vogel. Do you remember I was telling you I thought I could prove I had ripped my jacket somewhere else? Do you want to find that proof? Tonight?"

"If you know where it is, of course I do. You should have said something earlier...."

"Then we'll need to make a slight side trip," Felix said. "But I promise it won't take long."

"You'd better not be wasting my time, Page," Vogel told him sharply. "If I find that you are, heaven help you!"

Laura looked up to see Gordon and Janice walking toward them. In contrast to her father, she was dressed in a brilliant forest green outfit that complemented her flame-red hair and green eyes perfectly. She looked through and past Laura, as she glanced casually at the lieutenant.

"I think I'll join the fun," she said. "I haven't been to the Apocalypse police station since I was a child on a field trip."

"You'd be welcome at most any other time, Miss Ulric," Vogel said. "But you'd only be a distraction tonight."

"I insist that my daughter be allowed to accompany me," Gordon put in. I don't want her calling my attorney from El Norte. Someone may overhear her. I want her to call him from the station."

"All right then, Miss Ulric," Vogel shrugged. "If you want to ride with us into town I certainly won't stop you."

"Of course not—*Lieutenant*—" Janice drawled, the unspoken threat against Vogel's job hanging in the air. "I'll ride with my father."

"If I remember correctly, you and Mr. Page were engaged to be married at one time," Vogel continued, as if she hadn't spoken. "Why, yes, Miss Ulric, I think you'll fit in with our little group quite well...."

"Then we're agreed. Good!" Janice smiled at Felix, ignoring Laura. "May we use my car?" she added, gesturing toward a large sedan parked near the front of the building.

"I'm afraid not," Vogel said. "Unless you prefer to drive by yourself, Miss Ulric. The rest of us will be taking my car."

"Oh, well, all right," Janice pouted, looking in disdain at Vogel's less than pristine mode of transportation. Laura noticed that even as she made the face, Janice was beautiful.

Vogel pushed open the door and a brisk wind touched them. Janice, the last one to leave the hall, responded indifferently when she was reminded to fasten the door firmly behind her. In the end, Gordon went back and did it himself.

Felix seemed apprehensive. "What's wrong?" Laura whispered.

"This wind is likely to make it more difficult to retrieve the evidence," Felix said.

"What do you mean?"

Vogel, at Felix's side, interrupted them. "Let's not borrow trouble, Page. I want to get this settled as much as you do. Just tell me where you need to go...."

Janice looked dismayed at the prospect of sitting on the stained graying seat covers in her stylish outfit. But soon she settled herself comfortably in the back and opened the ash tray in front of her. "Does anyone mind if I smoke?"

"Nobody in my family smokes," Vogel said. "So I'd prefer if you didn't." He turned to Felix and asked, "All right, Page. Where to?"

"The bridge," Felix said. "The bridge where Oscar Clymer was killed."

"Is that where you claim you tore your jacket sleeve?"

"I *did* rip the damn thing there. I wanted to see for myself if the so-called dangerous bridges of El Norte could be made any safer. To see for myself, I went out to the place where Clymer was shot. While I was looking at the spot from which the man had fallen, my *left* jacket sleeve tore on a chunk of the railing wood and a piece of the material was caught there."

"And you think that piece of cloth might still be there?"

"If the wind hasn't blown it away, yes."

"Then we'll go have a look before we go to the station." Vogel began backing his car out. "I don't want it to be said that I didn't give you every possible chance to clear yourself, Page."

Vogel was quiet during the drive. Janice, an inveterate back-seat driver, kept up a nonstop monologue.

Laura again gazed out the window at the beauty of El Norte. Even late at night, it seemed to have a personality. There was such an aura of wilderness; of unexplored lands that remained unobserved by human eyes; yet at the same time, there was the certain knowledge of not being too far from the comfort and safety of home. To Laura, it was like a microcosm of her own life, of all the difficulties and hardships, the fears and the joy that had led her to Coralton—and into the safe harbor of Felix's arms.

"Here we are," Vogel said a short time later. "Let's check it out." He grabbed a flashlight out of the glove compartment and bent its fading yellow eye on sand, wood, and on a point near one end of the bridge where a large hole in the railing had been left unrepaired.

"You can come out and help me look," Vogel said to Felix. "I don't want it to be said I was unfair."

Laura got out of the car, too, behind Felix. The rear door opened and she knew that Gordon had stepped out as well. She started to ask Vogel whether he approved of letting Ulric so close to evidence which might exonerate Felix; but it seemed better for her to stay near Felix and keep a low profile.

"Well?" Vogel played his flashlight along the railing and over the hole at the end. "I don't see anything hanging there."

"You're right." Felix had his hand on the wood. The sand grated under his feet. "It must have happened when I was getting close to the end of the bridge—with my eyes fixated on the hole and nothing else. I know I tore my jacket near here; that much I know for a fact—Laura, what in the world is wrong?"

Laura had gasped. She had turned briefly to keep an eye on Gordon as he walked behind them along the railing. He was moving slowly, both hands on the wood, testing it carefully before he took the next step. There was a snag in the wood at one point, and he hissed when his fingers touched it; the sound had riveted Laura's attention firmly on him. Then he let out a sigh and his fingers moved rapidly over the edge of the snag. He made a motion as if he were extracting something from the wood or drawing something away from it.

Laura ran to him as quickly as she could, but his fingers were already raised aloft. A grimace of satisfaction gleamed clearly in the cold light of the nearly-full moon.

Vogel called out. "What are you doing?"

"Gordon was looking for the piece of cloth. And he found it! I know he found it. I could see...and then he threw it away!" The flashlight in Vogel's hand played across her and she panto-mimed Gordon's gestures with her own fingers. Behind her one of the car doors suddenly slammed shut and Janice's high heels clattered on the bridge.

"What the hell's going on?" she called out. "You didn't found anything, did you?"

"That really *would* be a setback; wouldn't it?" Laura said angrily.

Felix looked into Gordon's face, nodded and caught Vogel's eye. "He did it all right. I've known him forever, and I can tell from his face that he's done something questionable."

Gordon blinked into the light. "Lieutenant Vogel, can you think of any possible reason why I should want to put this boy's life and reputation in jeopardy?"

"Sure, I can," Vogel nodded. "Just so long as he's in trouble with the police, he won't be able to stand in the way of your putting up those apartment buildings you're so crazy for. I'm equally sure you've convinced yourself that some other proof will turn up in time to save him—after your building project has gone forward, that is."

Ulric stiffened and lowered his eyes. Other than that, he said not a word in denial.

Laura turned to Vogel. "And isn't it possible that he might have been responsible for Oscar Clymer's death himself, somehow, and is trying to make sure somebody else gets the blame for it."

"Does my father have to listen to this nonsense?" Janice asked the lieutenant.

Laura ignored her, "Or, maybe he knows who did it and wants to protect *that* person because he—or she," she glared at Janice, "is very close to him."

"Hold on a minute, Mrs. Page," Vogel said as Janice gasped. "I understand that you feel as if your husband is in a great deal of trouble, and you want to put everybody else in the same boat; but that isn't an easy task, in a case like this. The fact is that you and your husband would appear to be the only two people on this bridge with Clymer when he fell—or was pushed over."

"He was shot before he fell," Laura insisted.

"Then how do you explain the fact that there was no bullet wound on the body. According to the final portmortem—"

Laura's head whipped up. "Yes. That was what you told Felix and me when you said you were waiting for results from the *complete* examination—to know whether or not Felix strangled Oscar. This is as good a time as any, Lieutenant Vogel. You should know perfectly well by now that *Felix never hurt that man*! Don't you, Lieutenant? *Don't you?*"

Vogel glanced at the Ulrics then wiped his mouth slowly with the back of a hand.

"Why are you keeping the findings a secret?" Laura insisted. "The portmortem results *have* to clear Felix of the murder, and I think you should say so to the people who are trying to destroy Felix, and who don't give a damn what they do to me in the process, either."

"Lieutenant, I want to sue this woman for slander," Janice

snapped. "And I want to take out the papers right now, or as soon as is humanly possible."

Gordon waved a hand tiredly. "Pay no attention to any of this, Janice."

"And by the way—while we're discussing despicable behavior—this man wrote me a letter," Laura said. "But he addressed it so that Felix was led to open it first. It was worded in a way calculated to drive Felix into a fit of anger and break us up!"

Vogel smacked a fist into a palm. "Now all this has to stop, and I mean it. I'm not about to stand here listening to all this yelling and accusations out here in the middle of the night."

Laura felt Felix had touched her gently, but still she spoke out again, after a moment's silence, and almost as if Vogel hadn't spoken.

"We came here to find some evidence to help my husband, but now it's been deliberately destroyed—by Gordon—and practically under your nose, Lieutenant."

Vogel was angry. He clicked the flashlight impatiently on and off, on and off, to relieve his frustrations.

"I, for one, don't believe the so-called evidence ever existed," he said finally. "And I'm not absolutely sure that Mrs. Page saw Mr. Ulric throw it away, deliberately or not, a few minutes ago. In fact, Mrs. Page, I think you're nothing more or less than a hysterical woman."

"Thank you, Lieutenant," Gordon said smugly, at having been vindicated. "Your confidence in me is deeply gratifying."

"I have a suggestion that may be of some help." Janice said coolly.

Gordon turned to her, "Janice, I do wish you wouldn't interf—discuss this matter—until we're back at home."

"My suggestion," Janice said firmly ignoring him, "would be to give this woman a chance to prove her husband's innocence—at least his innocence of having tried to do her any harm earlier tonight. That is, of course, if she wants to risk it."

Laura turned toward Janice warily. She had never looked

lovelier than she did tonight, with that flicker of wind playing with her vibrant red hair. Her skin glowed; she seemed *carelessly* beautiful, rather than as if she had been tended to with studied care. All the love in Janice Ulric's being, Laura realized, had been spent on Janice herself.

"I understand there's a trick to it," Laura said, "but let me hear what you have in mind. Then I'll decide."

Once she felt she had everyone's undivided attention, Janice continued. "This material is missing. I mean, of course, the threads torn from Felix's jacket. What I would suggest is that *she* go look for them."

"What?" Vogel asked, as if he could not have heard her correctly.

"Well—right here on the bridge, for a start." Janice pointed past the railing and added, "then down there, in the canyon. You never know where the wind might have carried that little piece of wool, but it couldn't have been carried too far, do you think?"

"There's no point in playing games, Miss Ulric," Vogel said. "You know perfectly well that it would be practically impossible to find anything that small down there in the dark. All that would happen is that Mrs. Page here would be made uncomfortable from the exertion and, perhaps, even endanger herself. I'm not going to allow such a thing just to indulge you in a personal act of spite."

"I resent that!" But before she could be stopped, Janice had grabbed the flashlight out of Vogel's hand and lowered it so that the light shone, somewhat uselessly, across the sandy expanse below the bridge.

"It certainly isn't so much to ask of a loyal little wife is it? Why, I know that if I were married to Felix—not that I'd go through with marriage to a man who's got such an awful temper—but if I *had* married him, I wouldn't hesitate for a minute to get dirty—if it meant even a slight chance to—"

Felix cleared his throat and Laura was reminded that they had been talking past the one person among them who had so much to lose. Felix followed the flashlight beam with his eyes to its destination.

"Let's do it!" he said suddenly.

"What are you talking about?" Vogel growled.

"Search down there." Felix pointed into the sandy canyon beneath them.

"Are you crazy?" Vogel thought hard for a moment. "All right, Page. I swore I'd give you every break possible. First, though, before we do another thing, give me your jacket. The torn one."

Felix complied silently. Vogel stretched it across the railing as carefully as he could, flashing the light over every inch of it. Finally he nodded in satisfaction and folded it over his left arm. "No new rips in it. Page, if you try to pull a fast one, at least you can't claim you just found some material you just tore off the jacket."

Felix had already started toward the end of the bridge when Vogel called out:

"Mr. Ulric, I want you and your daughter to stay inside the car...."

Janice puffed up angrily, "Of all the damned silly—"

Vogel addressed himself to Ulric: "I don't want to hear you or your daughter making any more remarks while Page and I are down there conducting the search. In fact, I don't want to hear the sound of her voice at all—or yours."

Gordon drew up stiffly. "I don't believe for a moment that my daughter is out to cause some kind of mischief."

"Well, that's where I differ with you. In my opinion, she's not only out for mischief, but she's succeeding at it." Vogel sniffed disapprovingly. "I said I want you two to stay in the car—and I mean it."

As he followed their progress back into the car with his flashlight, Laura couldn't help but notice that the light had become dim, indicating a weakening of the batteries.

"All right," Vogel said at last. "Let's get this over with. Mrs. Page, you'd better come with us. I don't want to leave you alone up here on the bridge."

The strong winds continued shifting the sand, swirling and whirling about as they descended into the abyss. Felix held Laura's arm to guide and steady her, in spite of his eagerness to reach the floor of the canyon as quickly as possible. More than once Laura felt the area on which she was standing shift and slide out from under her; and it took a certain amount of dogged persistence on her part to keep from communicating her anxiety and distress.

At last they stood at the bottom of the canyon, and several minutes later Vogel, the flashlight's yellow beam bouncing in front of him, followed suit,

"Now," Felix said to him, "let *me* have the flashlight, please, before it burns out. I need as much light as possible." He ran the thin line of light along the gritty sand. "The wind is playing havoc here, but I know I saw something just a few minutes ago that gave me an idea."

"How is it possible you could have seen anything that we didn't...?" Vogel began.

"The wind must have uncovered it after we started down. Just give me a minute to look...." Felix edged out in a circular track, pausing from time to time to bend down and examine the sand before venturing another step.

"Well?" Vogel called out impatiently. "Did you find anything?"

"I'm almost certain it—damn!"

The flashlight battery chose that moment to give out at last, plunging them into darkness, except for the moonlight.

Felix promptly descended to all fours and began moving his fingers gently through the sand. He muttered under his breath as he worked.

"What are you doing?" Laura asked. "Tell us so we can help you...."

"I was right! *I was right!*" Felix called out. He came back to them carrying something that looked like a small flat piece of cardboard in his right hand. His left hand was clenched tightly to his chest.

"Please take charge of these, Lieutenant," he said, handing the items over.

"What are these?" Vogel asked. First the flat item in Felix's right hand was transferred. Vogel poked at it gingerly. "It looks like an old rubber ball squeezed flat—oh, I see—this must be the ball Clymer was experimenting with before he died. Are you telling me that you spotted it down in the sand from all the way up there on the bridge—in the dark?"

"Not exactly. What I saw was this other thing, laying on top of it, glittering in the moonlight, and it made me curious...."

It was a contact lens. Vogel took it into his free hand as if he expected the thing to blow up, like one of Clymer's practical jokes.

"You should be able to check to see if it matches Clymer's prescription," Felix said. "I think this may be the proof of what really happened to Clymer that evening."

"I think you're absolutely right," Vogel said slowly. "But not in the way you mean. In fact, Page, I think you've just sealed your own fate."

Felix was too shocked to answer. He stood open-mouthed, waiting to hear what conclusion Vogel had drawn from the evidence.

"You're smart, my friend," Vogel went on. "But it's always a mistake to try to fool a professional. Now you're going to tell me, I'm sure, that after you all heard the mythical gunshots on the bridge, Clymer was startled and dropped the rubber ball, He then, for some unexplained reason, lost his balance and fell through the railing to the canyon floor below, breaking his neck in the process. Next you're going to claim this rubber gizmo fell over at the same time, and Clymer's contact lens just happened to pop out of his eye and fall on top of it—all at the same time! But now you've found it and everything's dandy. Well, you might get a jury to go along with that—*if* you've got an exceptionally good lawyer backing you. But me? I don't buy it for a minute!"

Felix shook his head in frustration. "No! No! That's not what

I meant at all!"

Laura leaned toward him. "Tell Lieutenant Vogel what you had intended to tell him, Felix. *Please!*"

"Suppose you let me finish, first." Vogel said. "You really overreached yourself by 'finding' this, my friend. All this means is that you, and you alone, had the opportunity to take it out of Clymer's pocket when you came down here to 'inspect' the body. And, of course, you could easily have popped out one of his contact lenses and planted them together in the sand, to be found miraculously at a later date. But it just doesn't add up—and I'll prove it to you."

Felix waited. "Go ahead...."

"Your wife asked me about the final postmortem results. It just so happens that Clymer's neck *was* broken by the fall; but that isn't the good news you might think it is. You see, the clothing that Oscar Clymer was wearing at the time of his death was gone over carefully, as well. Some of his pockets were inside out when he was found, as if he'd been searched previously."

"His pockets may have been turned out from the force of the fall. I noticed that some of his pockets seemed to have been turned out when I first came down to examine the body," Felix began reasonably.

"But there's also a partial rip at the back of his jacket—and we recovered fingerprints—your prints, my friend."

"I probably touched him while we were walking together or when I felt for his heartb—" Felix snapped two fingers. "No, I remember now. I reached for him as he was falling; that must be how my prints got on Clymer's clothing—isn't that right, Laura?" He turned to her eagerly.

"And I'm sure your wife will back you up, as usual," Vogel said icily. "Now that you've told her what her story should be."

"But it's the truth!" Felix insisted. "I didn't push the man over or rig up a story afterwards. I'm almost certain now that what happened to Clym—"

Felix's words trailed off as he realized Vogel was still looking skeptically at him.

"But why do both of you keep on insisting that you heard gunshots, when you know damn well there's no trace of any bullets?" the lieutenant said after a pause. "I guess we'll have to save that for the questioning. Instead of jumping out of the frying pan, I believe you've landed yourself right back in the fire."

CHAPTER SIXTEEN

The first haze of dawn had begun to appear in the sky when Vogel's old car drew up in front of the antique elegance that was the Coralton estate.

Felix was adamant. "I won't have those two in the house," he said, gesturing in the direction of the Ulrics.

Vogel turned to Gordon and Janice. "I'm sorry, folks, but if you don't mind waiting here, I don't think this will take long. As soon as Mr. Page can get some clothes together—and calls his lawyer, we can all be on our way back to Apocalypse."

Laura opened the front door and Felix followed her in. They heard Vogel's footsteps behind them, as the lieutenant hurried to catch up.

In the dimly-lit hallway, Laura said quietly: "Let's not make any noise and wake—"

"Laura! Felix!" It was Selina's voice. "Come into the summer room—instantly!"

Felix turned around to get Vogel's agreement and the lieutenant nodded. "Might as well get this over with," he said. He stayed behind them as they walked in.

Harvey had been sitting next to his mother, patting her hand and speaking to her in low tones. He stood up at the sight of Laura and Felix, grinning from ear to ear.

"It's a good thing you're back, that's all I can tell you," he said. "I've been having kittens here, worrying about you two. Anything can happen when you're in a car, and you might not be found for hours."

Felix smiled at his brother, but Selina had become rigid in anger at the sight of Vogel.

Felix turned to her. "Looks like I'm under suspicion for having killed Oscar Clymer after all. I've got to call the lawyer."

Selina glared at the lieutenant. "My son didn't do anything, and you can't arrest him."

Fingers of sunlight streaming through the easternmost windows touched Vogel's tired gray face. He blinked. His jaw was set, tight and hard.

"Mrs. Page, I have a job to do and your son is under arrest. Give me some evidence to show that he's innocent, and I'll forget about taking him in."

Laura turned to her husband. "Felix, what did you think of while we were out there? I know you had something on your mind, but you couldn't bring yourself to tell it to the lieutenant. Well, you're in your own home now, and with the people who are closest to you. I know there was some idea that had occurred to you, and I think we should hear it now."

"Tell us," Selina ordered.

But Felix didn't respond to her immediately. Instead, smiling tentatively, he turned to Laura.

"The reason I didn't say anything when we were out there earlier, is that I can't be sure if my notion is any good until I check it out with somebody."

"With whom?"

He touched Laura's hand reassuringly then looked around the room. His eyes narrowed as they moved past his mother and stopped on his brother's smiling face.

"Harvey, there's something I need to ask you," he said.

Vogel interrupted. "He's no good as a witness. He'll say whatever you want him to say."

"Listen to me, Harvey," Felix said, his voice rising above the lieutenant's. "You're an inventor with patents to your credit— and I'm an architect, but we both know something about minia- turization. Right?"

"Correct," Harvey nodded vigorously.

"Now, I know that it's possible to make smaller items do the work that was previously done by much larger pieces," Felix continued carefully. "Transistors for example...can you think of any others?"

"Oh! There are *lots* more," Harvey said with a smile. "For inst—"

"Hear me out first, Harvey, because I might get mixed up if I don't proceed with my thought. What I'd *really* like to know is: do you think it would be possible to take a—oh—a rubber ball, for instance. Just a plain rubber ball, and change it somehow so that it could be crushed and later spring back to its usual shape?"

Lieutenant Vogel intervened. "Look here, Mr. Page. Just what are you trying to say?"

"Well, Harvey?" Felix ignored Vogel. "What do you think? Would it be possible to make something like that?"

"Oh, I'm sure it would." Harvey smiled at his brother conspiratorially. "I won't tell you how to do it right now, Felix." He looked around the room at the others. "But I'm sure I could do it—if you gave me a little time."

"If you ask me, he'd be sure that horses could fly as well," Vogel grunted.

"One other little thing, Harvey...." Felix continued to ignore the lieutenant. "Let's just suppose that you wanted to, say, construct a practical joke...the kind Mr. Clymer used to sell. Would it be possible to take that rubber ball and fix it up in such a way that, after it's been crushed a few times, it might suddenly shock the hell out of everyone by sounding as if several gunshots had been fired? Could a very tiny transistor placed inside, for instance, do that?"

Harvey practically jumped up and down with glee. "Of course, Felix! Of course it could. *I* could do something like that...!"

Vogel's face had turned from gray to red in a split second. "Look here, Page. This doesn't mean a thing. No matter what he says. And even if you're right about your brother making such a device resulting in Clymer losing his balance from surprise—that still doesn't get you off the hook for strangling Clymer. There's no hard evidence against anybody else. Motive and opportunity are key in this case. And they both work against you. And there's also one other point that makes your theory questionable."

"Wh—what is it!"

"You may be telling the truth about that crazy rubber ball, but what difference does that make? It proves nothing."

"But what about—?" Felix suddenly stopped short. He looked at Selina questioningly, as though he had just entered the room.

"Go on, dear," Laura urged him. "Go on with your thought."

Felix shook his head emphatically. "I haven't got another thing to say. Call the lawyer, Mother. I've made up my mind. I'm going with Vogel."

"No, wait, wait!" Laura shouted.

"What's wrong?" Harvey frowned anxiously at them both.

Lowering her voice to a normal pitch, Laura said: "Felix, you either know or suspect something. I believe you've just come up with the answer to the whole business. But why would you rather go to jail than tell us what it is?"

Felix whirled on her. "I don't want you to say another word on the subject, Laura. I mean it."

"Someone has to look out for your interests if you won't!"

"If you keep on with this, Laura, so help me, it will be the last time we ever see each other again, except in divorce court. I mean it, Laura. God help me, I mean it!"

Laura looked around the room in anguish. Selina, coldly furious, sat tapping her cane on the hardwood floor. Harvey was biting his lower lip in an effort to contain his emotions. Vogel sat stolidly apart from the others. Waiting to see what would happen next.

"You can say what you like, but I can't bear the thought of you in prison, Felix, for no good reason."

"If you continue with this, I guarantee you will be destroying whatever we have between us, Laura."

"We won't have anything at all if you're in prison—or worse." She turned away from him and looked at the sober-faced lieutenant. "Lieutenant Vogel. You may have heard that at my wedding there was some difficulty between Clymer and—and Harvey."

Felix turned and walked over to join his half-brother. Harvey smiled at the close contact, but politely gestured for silence as he listed with rapt attention to Laura.

"Harvey was badly humiliated at the wedding, and it was Clymer's fault; but Harvey decided to get even. He's a tinkerer, and he knew that Clymer personally tested every new item that looked promising. Harvey invented a rubber-like ball that could be crushed and would spring back to its natural shape again. He didn't tell anybody, of course, and he didn't say that after the ball had been crushed a certain number of times, it would lie flat and there would be the sound of gunshots. He sent it to Clymer anonymously, certain that Clymer would be shocked and possibly embarrassed in public when the shots were heard."

"Go on." Vogel's interest had definitely been caught. But Felix was murmuring to Harvey. It needed only a little of his persuasion before Harvey stood up and walked to the door. Felix was standing between Vogel and the door in such a position as to keep the lieutenant from making any move in that direction unless he wanted a direct collision.

"I asked him to get something for me," Felix said to Vogel. "He shouldn't have to be exposed to the foolishness we're listening to."

"He can always be brought back in—if that's necessary," Vogel acknowledged. His eyes hadn't left Laura since she had started to talk about Harvey Page.

Sadly she went on: "Harvey didn't expect what would happen in such a dangerous place when the shots had sounded out. Clymer was so startled that he lost his balance and fell, breaking his neck. Once he heard of Clymer's death, Harvey was too scared to come forward and tell us what he had done. The possible consequences must have upset him pretty badly. After all, even the idea of having to ride in a car into Apocalypse would come close to sending Harvey into a state of near collapse, if I'm any judge.

"At that point, I believe, Harvey turned against his brother when he realized that *he* could get the successful and brilliant Felix Page into serious trouble. Maybe he identified with Felix so closely that he wanted to play the part of Felix, and he put on a jacket that's a duplicate of Felix's—you can certainly check if he has a gray jacket like the one Felix is wearing now—and stole into my room that night...."

"You've explained that pretty well," Vogel conceded. "But I still don't understand why he would try to scare hell out of *you*? That doesn't seem to make sense."

Laura heard a muffled gasp, but didn't know from whom it had been drawn. Vogel was rigidly attentive, his lips taut. Felix looked everywhere but at her. Selina sat quietly with a bony hand covering her eyes.

Laura looked back again toward the door and hesitated, but said nothing about her notion that Harvey was on the other side, listening to what was being said in the room. "I'm not certain that I can explain Harvey's actions either," she said slowly.

"There are too many gaps in your suggestions to be convincing," Vogel said. "And what's more, there's at least one other point you simply can't explain away so easily."

"I'd like to hear what it is."

"Your interpretation is that Clymer's death was an accident, brought on indirectly by a malicious, but not illegal, practical joke. It may not have been a crime, technically speaking, but the whole idea is so bizarre that I believe a full investigation into all of these theories is necessary. Now, Harvey Page certainly realized that the crushed ball might be traced back to him soon after it was discovered. Careful police work might show that pieces of the device had been in his possession only a very short time ago. Are we agreed on this much?"

"You know more about police methods than I do," Laura acknowledged. "If you say so, I'm sure you're correct about that."

"Granted that your brother-in-law couldn't be accused of murder in such a situation, the most he would have had to fear would be a small local scandal, similar to the one his brother was subjected to recently. At the minimum, a public statement of culpability might need to be made—but I suspect that a man with Harvey's temperament would be desperately anxious to avoid just that sort of thing. And the only way he could be sure of that would be to destroy or hide the primary evidence. Agreed?"

"Yes, but—"

"All right, then, here's the point I'm getting at. We know that the shifting sand at the bottom of the canyon had covered over at least part of the evidence superficially. But what I want to know is: why didn't Harvey make some effort to destroy the evidence all the same. Why didn't he go out to the site to unearth the one piece of evidence which might give him some trouble in the future? It was absolutely insane to leave that crushed ball in the sand where it might be discovered eventually and, in my opinion, Harvey Page, in spite of his difficulties, is nowhere near that crazy."

"Yes, Lieutenant, I agree," Laura said slowly. "And that's the very point that gives Harvey away."

"You'll have to explain what you mean...."

Laura glanced at her husband. "Please explain it to him, Felix. Please do this one thing, at least, to save yourself...."

Felix turned his back on her and faced the door. From his stance, Laura knew he was weighing the logic of her request against his self-imposed obligation to his brother.

"It's up to you, then, I guess," Vogel said turning back to Laura. "You'll have to be the one to prove to me why your brother-in-law left incriminating evidence which might be found by someone else, and eventually find its way into police hands."

"Harvey *couldn't* go out to the canyon to search for the evidence." Laura told him in a flat and empty voice. "Ever since his accident many years ago, he's been absolutely terrified of automobiles, and he hasn't left Coralton or its grounds since he was a teenager. *That's* why Harvey had to leave the evidence there."

Vogel digested her statement in silence. "That makes sense," he agreed. "I'm sorry for him, but he will have to leave the house now and come downtown to give us an official statement. I suppose I could bring my people out here for a preliminary interview, but he'll be required to come in for any follow-up statements. And, for all I know, there may be some kind of legal action by the D.A.'s office, which would mean Harvey would need to appear at a court hearing—in town. I think you ought to start preparing him for what's almost certain to happen in the near futu—"

He was interrupted by the sound—from just outside the summer room—of a pistol shot.

Selina called out in anguish: "Harvey! Harvey! What have you done?"

Felix dashed through the door, Vogel close behind. Laura slipped through and slammed the door shut behind them to prevent her mother-in-law from seeing what surely awaited them in the hall.

Harvey Page lay flat on his back, arms outstretched, on the polished parquet floor. His eyes were wide open, staring blankly into nothingness. The weapon grasped tightly in his right hand was no larger than a fountain pen, but it had made a blood-streaked hole in his right temple. There was no doubt in Laura's mind that the toy-like device was one of the inventions with which he had been tinkering in the cellar. There was a vague scent near his face that reminded Laura of gasoline.

Vogel bent over him, feeling for a pulse. When he looked up, he was shaking his head gravely. He glanced toward the summer room, and sighed with relief at seeing that the door had been closed. But he shook his head as the sound of Selina's cane tap-tapping on the floor, brought her nearer to learning what her son had done to himself.

So yet another Page has fallen victim to a calamity of his own making, Laura thought sadly. And here we all are...left to deal with it however we can....

"My fault," Vogel said quietly. "I thought I heard him on the other side of the door. I shouldn't have talked so much about the difficulties awaiting him."

"No. It was *her* fault," Felix said bitterly, gesturing at his wife.

"But I *had* to—" Laura began.

"Harvey's killed himself...because of you. I suppose now you're satisfied!"

He turned abruptly and waited for his mother to open: the door. Selina Page, gray-faced and walking with more difficulty than usual, made her way painfully to the scene of her son's self-inflicted death. Laura, watching her in sympathy, felt certain that the events of the last few moments would assure the demise of her marriage. She had been successful in protecting her husband from prison and scandal, but by doing it, she had probably lost him forever.

CHAPTER SEVENTEEN

Nobody had to order Laura to pack this time.

She did it alone as the blazing sun rose to its morning zenith—nearly blinding her when its rays reached in through the open windows of her room on the second floor of the old mansion she had come to call home. During the few weeks of her marriage she had accumulated so many additional items of clothing and memorabilia that she scarcely knew where to tuck them into the cavernous corners of her largest suitcase. Her whole life had taught her that material things should be thought of as transitory, but that her marriage to Felix should have been on the same level was almost impossible for her to accept.

And yet....

Hadn't she come here, in a way, under false pretenses? Hadn't she been seeking security more than anything else? She had built her entire previous life on a desire for stability, even going into a profession that was taken for granted as a stepping stone to a comfortable marriage. She was, in fact, no better than any other social climber. It was purely by accident that her affection for Felix should have become so warm and real and that she now knew she loved him completely—and always would.

Fighting back the tears, she turned away in resignation from the sight of her bridal gown and veil, cleaned and packed away in an archival box, and stored on the upper shelf of her closet.

The ringing phone kept her from a fresh outburst of sobs. It was Jack Noland.

"I'm calling Felix's personal line because I've got a message for him," Noland said, after inquiring after Laura's well-being and responding politely to her non-committal answers. "Have him call me right away. Tell him it's about his propositions for saving El Norte. Tell him that the news of his having been cleared of murder has gotten around very quickly—and it's making a difference to his neighbors."

Laura managed to hang up without having discuss anything further about the morning's events to Jack. She didn't want to disturb the servants, who were all busily involved dealing with the tragedy and its aftermath. She quickly wrote out Jack's message on a piece of paper arid took it downstairs.

She planned to leave it conspicuously on Felix's desk, where it wouldn't be missed. On her way there, however, she heard Selina's voice behind a closed door of one of the salons, and her words were clear and unequivocal.

"...feel just as badly as you do about what happened. Worse, I'm sure. What they say about a mother's love, Felix, isn't at all exaggerated."

Laura heard Felix's mumbled voice without being able to make out what he was saying. The knowledge that he was so close to her caused Laura to tremble violently.

"In all fairness, Felix, Laura worked tirelessly for you and in your behalf. Nothing else can be more important, as far as you're concerned."

To hear Selina take her side so vehemently seemed impossible to Laura on this dreadful day.

"Yes, even against *me*," Selina went on. "A woman who acts for you against the whole world is the one person you shouldn't let go."

They were in the Spanish salon, Laura realized. She knocked softly on the door and, without waiting for a response, turned the handle and entered. Selina was perched on one of the little antique chairs. Felix, standing nearby, whirled around when she came in, his eyes blazing at her in challenge.

"You've had a phone call from Jack Noland," Laura said calmly, handing him the message. "It's about your future plans for El Norte."

Without a word, he wheeled around and went out to return the call. The women waited in silence until he returned a few minutes later. He said nothing to Laura, but she was filled with joy as he spoke earnestly to Selina.

"They want *me* to go to Jacksonville after all, to make the case before the State Highway Commission." Felix said, "I'm to follow my original plans for controlled expansion, but to add that we want zoning laws to keep the number of new houses down, and to keep those that are built clustered together—which is what Oscar Clymer was suggesting, by the way. And I told Jack I'd recommend that any new houses shouldn't be more than two-stories—and that all new structures should be constructed only where they can't interfere with the natural skyline."

Laura couldn't help breaking in: "Jack and the others were so impressed to hear you last night at the public rally that they couldn't turn to anyb—"

She had said the wrong thing again, or perhaps anything she said would have been wrong. Felix was looking at her as if she were a stranger.

"I know it isn't everything you wanted, Felix," Selina said with surprising reasonableness. "But it's possible that we simply don't have the right to keep other people out of El Norte."

Felix seemed unable to look away from the sight of his wife. Noticing his preoccupation, Selina got to her feet suddenly.

"Remember, Felix, what I just told you," she said, and left the room abruptly. They could hear the tap of her cane along the hallway for some moments after the door had been closed.

"Harvey wasn't as mentally confused as you tried to make him out to be when you told that story to Vogel," Felix said suddenly. "Harvey tried to scare you like that because he'd been asked to do it by somebody to whom he felt loyalty. I got the truth from Gordon Ulric before he and Janice and Vogel left."

Laura wanted to ask him for whom Harvey would feel such loyalty—but at the same time she was finding it difficult to speak, and she felt sure that her voice wouldn't sound even remotely normal.

Luckily, Felix answered the unspoken question.

"Harvey was doing what *Gordon* asked him to do—give you a damned good scare that could be blamed on me. He did it for two reasons: in the first place, it was hard for him to say no to anybody he liked—and in the second place, Gordon Ulric is his uncle."

"His—his uncle?" Laura tried to keep her voice from revealing her shock.

"Yes. Gordon's late brother was my mother's first husband—and Harvey's father," Felix said. "You've been told that everybody in El Norte has known each other for a long, long time. As a result, we've got a certain loyalty to each other—and many of us are related, by blood or marriage."

Laura answered the real accusation in his words.

"But you think I was disloyal because I helped *you*, instead of Harvey," she said. "I don't agree with you, but I'm tired of having one long argument after another about it."

"What does that mean?"

"Only that I'll be glad, in one way, to be leaving."

"You know what my mother thinks?" he asked. "Her notion is that I ought to grab you by the hair until you agree to stay."

"Thank her for finally wanting me at Coralton, Felix; but I don't want to see her again before I leave."

"I don't think that the two of you could ever be good friends, but at least now I know she appreciates you," Felix said. "I don't agree with my mother about what she wants, though, and it's my life we're talking about—not to mention yours."

"Very well, Felix, I understand that things are finished between us. A boy I used to know once said to me that there are happy beginnings in a relationship, and there can be happy middles in a relationship, but there are never any happy endings."

"You *want* to go, don't you?" he asked.

She hesitated. "Under the circumstances, I think I must."

"Before you left earlier, Laura, I'd gone upstairs to talk to you."

"About a divorce?" She picked her words carefully. "I'll start an action as soon as I get back to New York, if that's what you want."

"That's up to you," Felix said. "I can't stop you from doing it, if you've made up your mind."

She wanted to tell him then that he could stop her with the flick of an eyelash or the waggle of a finger. Being forced to stand ten feet away from him and look at those fine features she knew so well was a special torture, unlike any to which she had ever before been exposed.

"Well, then, Felix, that's all, I guess," she said after a brief silence. "Goodbye."

"No, wait."

"Is there something I've forgotten? I'll leave all the keys with Susan before I go."

"Damn it, Laura, don't make things so hard for me!" he burst out.

"We're making things hard for each other," she said quietly. "It'll be better if I go as soon as possible."

"Just let me say one thing before you go."

"Of course, Felix."

But the torture of being so close to him and yet being treated like a stranger was likely to stretch out until her nerves would be crushed like eggshells in a huge fist.

"I think that what has happened to us in the last few weeks has done a lot to tame my temper," he said finally. "That may sound crazy to you, Laura, but I mean it. To know that I was suspected of murder and that you were given a rough time by someone so close to me—only because I'm known for my bad temper—well, as I say, it's enough to make any man think twice about himself, and decide that he can't make a success out of his life unless he puts some changes in affect—as soon as possible."

Laura said, "I agree with you. And I feel sure that you won't be so vulnerable to such violent reactions in the future,"

"Thank you, Laura, and I know you mean it. But that isn't all I wanted to say."

Laura, having turned to go, made herself look back at him. She couldn't remember how many times she had held that chin against her palm, but the memory was painfully vivid.

"I know you can hardly wait to get out of my sight, Laura, but we did have something good between us not too long ago, and for that reason alone, I'm asking you to be patient a little longer. It's just that I'm trying to find the words. You know it's hard for me to say exactly what I want to."

"It was relatively easy for you at the rally last night," she smiled. "And I'm sure it won't be any harder for you at Jacksonville, even if you will be playing into Gordon's hands by what you tell the State Commission."

His head snapped back. "I won't be doing Gordon Ulric any favors! He wanted to put up big buildings and now he won't be able to."

"No, but he will be able to put up a few houses, and with your agreement."

"He will not," Felix said positively. "Gordon's land is positioned so that he couldn't put up an outhouse without its interfering with the skyline of El Norte, and I specifically made a point of saying that no structures interfering with the skyline would be allowed. And the sandy nature of the land is such that he can't hope to blast away and level it without—oh, forget about Gordon! We're alone for the last time in months, maybe, and we don't have to stand here and talk about Gordon or his daughter."

Laura promptly echoed, "'We're alone for the last time in months, maybe.' I thought that we were alone for the last time, period."

"I hope not. It seems to me that, instead of leaving El Norte, you ought to stay close by, as my mother wants, for a few more months, just to see if I'm right about my control being much better. And if I am right, we could be together again. That is, of course, if you still want to be with me."

Laura could remember only vaguely that she had recently contemplated leaving Coralton forever, never expecting to hear one word of affection, real or implied, from Felix Page. And in time, she knew, that vague recollection would be swept out of her mind, as if it had never existed.

"Then you're suggesting that I wait for you," she said carefully, "until you're sure that it's all right to be with me again."

"You make it sound as if I'm sick, Laura. I know I've got a rotten temper, but I also know I'm not crazy."

"You just gave me a little lecture on loyalty, Felix, if you recall. You told me that Harvey acted against his own wishes, because he felt loyal to his uncle. But my loyalties are less complicated than that. You're the only person I want to be with; the only person I want to help, the only one to whom I need to be loyal."

"Then you *will* wait for me," he said, smiling slowly. "Laura, I promise you won't regret it."

"I won't spend a day waiting," Laura said. "I'm going to do exactly what your mother wants me to do. I'm staying. I'll be right here at Coralton."

"But you mustn't do that. I'm liable to—well, I know I won't. But how can we both be sure?"

"When I was upstairs a few minutes ago, packing my clothes," Laura said, "I told myself that I had married you mainly because I wanted to be secure, and that it was only a matter of luck that I had fallen in love with you. But that isn't really true, I think I was telling myself a story, a fairy tale, to make me feel better— only a little better—about leaving here. It was my particular 'out,' so to speak."

"And you think I'm telling myself a different kind of story to justify—what?"

"A 'vacation' from marriage, which you don't really want any more than I'd look forward to leaving Coralton."

"It isn't a matter of wanting to or not." Felix said. "There is no choice."

"You can take me with you to Jacksonville as part of that honeymoon we haven't had yet," Laura said, her eyes sparkling. "If you want to pitch in and make this marriage work, dear, we can do it together. And we will, Felix. I know that now."

"But look here," Felix said, coming closer to her and taking her hands in his at last. "You do need physical security at the very least, whether you admit it or not, Laura. That's one of the reasons a woman gets married."

"You're right, of course, in a way."

"Well, then, you shouldn't want to spend the rest of your life with a man who might just possibly haul off once in a very great while and let you have it."

"But *I'm* sure now you won't."

"So am I, actually, now, Laura. But you can't be a hundred percent sure. Why do you want to take the chance?"

"There are more important things in the world than certainty," said Laura Page *neé* Foster, as she snuggled down, safe at last, in her husband's arms.

ABOUT THE AUTHOR

EVELYN BOND is the author of some ninety novels, including mysteries, science fiction, romances, gothics, and many others, a number of which are being reprinted by the Borgo Press. She lives and works in New York.

www.ingramcontent.com/pod-product-compliance
Lightning Source LLC
Chambersburg PA
CBHW050732250626
47155CB00005B/1758